With Her This Christmas

A Holiday Novella

Hildred Billings

BARACHOU PRESS

With Her This Christmas

Copyright: Hilded Billings
Published: 7th December, 2020
Publisher: Barachou Press

This is a work of fiction. Any and all similarities to any characters, settings, or situations are purely coincidental.

Chapter 1

The rain and time of year may have conspired to make Seaside the gloomiest city on the coast, but nobody glowed more than Abbie Greywood, one of the touristy town's locals.

That title was earned, too. Abbie hadn't grown up in Seaside, perhaps considered the northern Oregon coast's most prominent town, but she had made a minor name for herself since she permanently moved into her family's beachfront vacation home. Four years ago, she had knocked on the neighbor's door and discovered a lonely elder of the community who was more than happy to give dear Abbie the connections she needed to get whatever she needed. Like a job! Thanks to one of Seaside's denizens, Abbie got a part-time job at one of the tourist shops by the promenade. Two years later, she was the manager. Now? She was practically an owner in everything but name.

Her coworkers loved her. Even the crotchety, sometimes more conservative business owners on the street respected her hard work ethic and shining personality that lit up every face. Men, both hardened locals and softer tourists, were quick to flirt with her in the hopes they might catch her fancy. Unfortunately for them, Abbie was gayer than the Pride flag she hung in her dining room window every June. Also known as the one big reason she was perpetually single.

Until recently. Kinda.

"Could you *please* finish locking up for me today?" she asked Sid, her only coworker hanging out with her in the shop that day. "I'm late enough as it is for my date, and it's gonna be a good one." She snuck a look at her phone. Sure enough, she had five missed texts from the woman she had been "seeing" since May. "Please, please, *please*."

Sid, who had been moving stock from a back room to the register desk, held up his hands in defeat. "Of course, Abs. Though you know I have to give you shit about your Zoom date, right? That's not a real date."

"Welcome to 2020!" Abbie flipped shut the notebook that soon went into a locked drawer beneath the register. "This is how people date now. It's not enough we meet on dating websites. We have to date only over the internet, too. Honestly, do you think it was any different before Covid? She lives in Portland."

A box of snow globes landed on the counter. "I feel like you would have met up by now in the 'before times.'" Yes, that included air quotes with his fingers.

"Kinda what keeps it hot when you think about it." Abbie flashed him an excited smile as she leaped over the counter and stuck the landing. Sid rolled his eyes. Before he got used to Abbie's exuberant energy, he used to panic that she was going to slam her feet into this display case or knock over that rack of screen-printed shirts, each one saying, *"SUNNY*

SEASIDE." Now, he was so used to her bullshit that he didn't think twice about ignoring her. "The forbidden aspect of a relationship, yo. We can't meet up because we might infect each other with cooties."

"According to Mitchell next door, it's really the An-tee-fuh cooties we have to watch out for. Every Portlander is infected." Sid pointed to his temple, implying the big brain energy in that deduction. "Then again, he thinks you're infected anyway because you have the gay."

"You'd think he'd be into it. I've seen his porn stash he leaves laying around his office."

"Same. So gross." Sid slipped behind the counter and opened the till. There had hardly been any sales, let alone by check or cash, but the till had to be counted before the owner stepped through the door in the morning. "Hey, do me a favor and tell your internet girlfriend that she should come to Seaside and blow Mitchell's mind. He thinks all lesbians wear flannel, cut their hair, and drive big trucks."

"Dude." Abbie zipped up her raincoat. "That's just an Oregonian woman."

"Bless you all! Good night! I'm out!"

While Sid's voice boomed through the empty store, Abbie's laughter followed her out of the door and onto the rainy sidewalk. She pulled up the hood on her rain jacket and made sure her phone was secured in her pocket. The splattering of rain against her face was nothing compared to the bite of the December night wind whipping from the ocean and clocking anyone daring to go for a walk at almost seven. *Damn wind is so quick and rain is so thick that I can't even see the Christmas lights.* People had been decking out their businesses and storefronts since November, but that past week saw a sudden spike in garlands, string lights, and Santa Clauses waving to people. Abbie walked by the year-round Christmas store and thought about the train that circled the shop for only a quarter. The occasional family burst out of the gelato business while others lined up for their reservations at one of Seaside's many fish and chips restaurants. The roar of the ocean thundered not so far away – whenever the wind whipped up like this, the ocean was likely to serenade a few people to sleep. Such was the case when Abbie dared to look up at the many terraces dotting hotels, apartment buildings, and vacation rentals. *I can always tell who isn't from around here.* There would be a man standing on the balcony, hand shielding his face as he called to his wife that, *"This is the real coast right here! Whew! Get the camera!"* while his wife huddled behind the sliding door with her robe wrapped comfortably around her.

Although Abbie wasn't from Seaside, it sure felt like home, in its own silly way.

There's no place like Seaside anywhere else on the coast. She had been all up-and down it through her life. Her family hailed from Eugene, a city at the bottom of the Willamette Valley, but they were beach people at heart. Her father's tech job kept him in the valley, but it also afforded them their second home in Seaside, which they had rented out in the off-season until Abbie asked if she could become its year-round caretaker in exchange for free rent.

Although it wasn't so free now. She paid for the utilities while her parents paid the mortgage and property taxes, but it was better than renting a cramped apartment somewhere else on her barely-above-minimum-wage salary.

Muscle memory turned her down the right street in the deep, dark of the Seaside night. Rain blotted out the streetlights, but the wind carried the sounds of a barking dog that had snuck out of the two-bedroom house only two blocks away from the beach.

"Sammy!" Abbie hurried to the gate separating her dog from the residential street. At that time of night, it might be next to impossible for a passing car to see the black and white border collie before it was too late. "What are you doing?" She put a hand on her dog's wet head as she opened up the gate and quickly shut it behind her again. "Come on! Let's get inside!"

Sammy was at the front door before Abbie knew which way was up. Unlocking her door, albeit beneath the coverage of her front porch, was akin to beating back the tourists when she was trying to open the store during peak summer season. As soon as the door opened,

Sammy was inside, clacking dirty paws against the hardwood floors like a happy dog.

"What the hell, Sams?" Abbie locked her door and tossed her hands into the air. Her incredulous look had no effect on her dog, however, who looked up at her with so much love that it was almost criminal. "How did you get out this time, huh? Did Casey leave the doggy door unlocked when she left earlier?" She referred to the neighbor down the street who popped in every evening to give Sammy a quick walk and make sure she had food in her bowl. Sometimes, Casey was in a hurry and forgot to lock the doggy door, which meant Sammy was often found rolling around in the dirt or barking at birds when Abbie finally made it home. During rainstorms like the one outside?

Oh, God. Oh, no. Here it came!

"Sammy!" Abbie shielded her face when Sammy let rip the rain droplets in her fur. The shaking of dog ears, fur, and collar tags accompanied the front-row spray Abbie received. Some mud landed on the walls. A trail of dirt had followed Sammy from the front door. The bedraggled dog may have been having the time of her life, but Abbie didn't have a moment to spare for this. She was already late for her date!

"Fuck." She whipped out her phone and opened her most recent chat window. *"Sorry I'm going to be a little later. My dog made a big mess while I was out. Pleaaaase wait for me!"* She put her phone away and immediately ripped off her rain gear to hang up by the front door. While droplets gathered on the floor, Abbie rushed into the kitchen and threw a TV dinner into the microwave. Her wet, soggy dog followed her from room to room, leaving tiny pawprints that Abbie would usually clean up right away, except she was in such a hurry to get to her bedroom that she decided to wait until later.

She dropped the hot TV dinner on her bedroom desk while changing into something a little more comfortable. Sweaters and jeans landed in the hamper. Sammy hopped up on the bed and made herself at home, panting in excitement while getting Wet Dog on the comforter. Abbie still didn't care. She was too busy unearthing a silk negligee from her dresser and a loose robe to go with it.

This wasn't only about comfort. She stole a bite of her dinner while brushing out her hair and attempting to make herself look somewhat presentable. While her internet girlfriend was used to seeing her in all manner of finery – including the aforementioned rain gear or, heaven forbid, sick day pajamas – tonight was different. Tonight was Friday night, the one night a week Abbie was guaranteed to have a good time on her laptop.

Finally, with a breath that urged her dog to go take a nap in the other room, Abbie sank into her desk chair and opened her laptop.

Two minutes later, she saw a familiar, beautiful face in their favorite chat window.

"There you are." Joyce, the only woman to make Abbie's heart flutter and her loins ache, was so drop-dead gorgeous tonight that she might as well have been promoting herself on TV. *Not sure what she's promoting, but I'd be buying it!* This was a woman who looked like a desirable model no matter what she wore, be it the baggy sweaters of fall or the cheap sundresses of summer. Abbie had been enjoying every style with great enthusiasm, but tonight? Like most of their Friday nights? *I can hardly stand it! Look at her!* Her eye may have been instantly drawn to that soft, wavy black hair that nestled against Joyce's throat, but it was the ruby red lingerie that kept Abbie's attention. Joyce never wasted a moment getting ready for these chat-dates. From the moment she and Abbie first video chatted back in late May, she had always been dressed up, with her make-up just so and her jewelry placed like she had somewhere important to go. *But she doesn't. I know she's been in that little apartment of hers for months.* Abbie had the freedom to go to work, the store, and walk her dog. Joyce didn't even have a dog. She had her 500sq foot apartment on the fourth floor somewhere on the edge of Portland and Beaverton. She had her groceries delivered and her work was completely done on the computer she now used to taunt Abbie with tits and ass.

Keeping her waiting was verboten. Abbie knew this. Oh, she might be punished for it!

"Hi, babe." Did Abbie look okay? Nobody could tell her house smelled like wet dog, right? Or that she had yet to shower? Or that her breath reeked of microwaved fried rice with too much soy sauce? "I'm *so* sorry that I'm late. I had to take a coworker's shift at the shop tonight and close up. Then I got home and my dog was out in the yard... in the rain..."

Joyce pursed her lips. Those lovely, kissable lips that Abbie could only imagine having in bed with her. *We've done all sorts of unspeakably sexy things, but I've still never touched her. Or kissed her!* One day, Abbie told herself, she would get to have actual in-person sex with this woman she had been fooling around with online for several months. One day. When it was safe!

"Don't worry about it," Joyce said, her teeth grazing her bottom, bitable lip. "I've been sitting here entertaining myself for a decent while. Don't ask me what I've been watching. Or doing." She leaned closer to her camera.

Soon, her face took up the whole screen. Was she about to leave lipstick behind? "Unless you're ready to relax a little. Did you get my package yet?"

"Oh. Right!" Abbie picked up the small box that had been by her desk since the day before. Joyce had told her to not peek until their Friday night chat. Abbie had already opened it, but she swore she didn't *peek*. She was saving that for this moment. "Can I look now?"

"Of course. I'm dying for you to finally pry that thing open."

With a grin the size of the squeal in her throat, Abbie ripped apart the packing paper and dug in. She didn't look at Joyce's reaction until a pair of lacey black panties were in her hand.

"Oh ho ho!" Abbie dangled the underwear in front of her webcam. "Is this what I think it is?"

"I told you I'd send them. Unwashed."

"I feel like I bought these from you or something. Am I one of your OnlyFans?" Abbie stretched Joyce's underwear between her hands, the ceiling light in the bedroom more diluted now that Abbie was tempted to let the panties drop upon her face. "You swear these were the ones you were wearing last week?"

"Honey, those panties are unwearable now. Especially since I didn't throw them in the wash. Hm. Come to think of it, I *should* have sold them instead of giving them away."

"Except they wouldn't mean the same to somebody else that they do to *meee*." Abbie would never forget the week before. Not the night Joyce sat in front of her webcam in nothing but this pair of underwear, touching herself until she forgot she was sitting in a chair with wheels. *Man, she almost fell out of that thing so many times when we started dating.* Joyce had a whole system now to ensure she never took off across the room or accidentally tipped her chair over when she was... busy. That was part of the foreplay for Abbie, who always had to contain her excitement as soon as Joyce braced her feet against the desk. "Don't suppose you included the vibrator you used, too."

"No, but if you stay on my nice list, I might send you your own for Christmas." Joyce tipped her head back with a smile, exposing the most vulnerable part of her throat. *One day. Hickey. Going right there.* "Keep looking in the box. Sooo many more goodies. Not all sexual!"

"But what if I only want the sexual ones?"

"Tough titties. Not everything's about sex, if you can believe it."

In quarantine, it might as well be. Abbie pulled back another piece of packing paper and found the local Portland coffee she had asked for Christmas. "Aw! Thank you! Were they able to deliver it to you?"

"No. I had to stop in and pick it up. I do that so rarely. It feels so weird standing in an empty café waiting for an order to be up. They told me I could order the beans online, but they were all sold out there. So it was me and a few other masked-up assholes waiting for coffee like it was 2019."

"Meanwhile, things here have hardly changed."

Joyce made a look that implied the entirety of Seaside was the reason Oregon kept going back into lockdown.

"That's not what I meant, all right?" Abbie set aside the package of coffee and looked back into the box. "Oh! Look! More sexual things!"

Joyce laughed. "I mean, I didn't say it wasn't *all* sexual. Only that not everything is sexual. Unless you think coffee is sexual."

"Dunno. Depends if you're using it sexually." Abbie held up a few Polaroids to the light. "This is so awesomely retro. How did you get the lighting to work like that?"

"Lots of boredom after work earlier this week. By the way, the dress is new in those pics. Do you like it? Maybe I'll wear it next week."

Liked it? *Liked it?* Abbie could hardly take her eyes off the slitty black dress Joyce wore in her selfies and carefully timed shots of her showing off her body like it was a professional centerfold from the '80s or '90s. When she did her makeup like that, she looked like she meant serious business on the seduction front. *Going straight for my pussy. I love it.* Oh, and Joyce was going for her pussy, too! Nice!

"Now don't keep those in your wallet." Joyce said that the moment Abbie unearthed the photo that was as gratuitous as a common porn shot. *Right out of the "amateurs" section.* At least the lighting was good enough that Abbie could make out the finger going God knows where. Honestly, she was distracted by the bare ass in the camera lens. "I don't need all of Seaside knowing what my pussy looks like."

"Your pussy deserves to be shown to everyone, though." Abbie shrugged. "Damn. How am I supposed to top this? I only have my phone. If I take porny nudes, they get uploaded to some cloud. If I ever get hacked, I won't have the chance to make money off them."

"But *I'll* have them."

"This is true. Let me think about it." Abbie neatly stacked the naughty Polaroids on the end of her desk and continued rooting through the package. "What else do we have in here? A lock of your hair? A baggy of your pubes?"

"Oh, stop."

"Whoa!" A handwritten card of instructions was soon in her hand. "What is it?"

"Let's say I couldn't send you a phone, so I told you what to do with yours."

"What the hell is 'Pleasure Blitz?' I'm scared to look it up."

"It's an app. Once you download it, I'll give you the code you need."

"I don't think this is the kind of app I need on my phone." Nevertheless, Abbie pulled over her phone and woke it up from its naïve slumber. "It's gonna be naughty."

"Don't worry. It's discreet. I've been using it for a while. Testing it out." Joyce's shoulders shook back and forth in anticipation. "Hurry up! This is what I've been waiting for."

"Okay, okay." A part of Abbie was shocked she found it on her app store. The summary didn't clear anything up, and the five star reviews merely said. "*Works great. Lots of fun!*" Here was hoping she wasn't signing away her data for something stupid. "It's downloading."

"All right. I'm gonna type the passcode in the chat. Can't wait."

"So, uh..." Abbie cleared her throat. "How have you been doing? We haven't had a chance to video chat since last Friday."

Joyce leaned back in her seat. *She's not wearing a thing under that piece of lingerie.* Not even underwear, bless her. "Things stay whatever. It being so dark so early and too rainy for a walk means I'm cooped up in here more than ever." She stretched her arms above her head, breasts heaving toward the camera. Abbie almost missed the part where the app finished downloading. *Can't exactly look away from a sight like this...* Joyce had a body to die for. The only time she really went outside was either to walk or run. Although her apartment was small, Abbie had a good view of the elliptical machine in the corner of the room. Between that and the yoga and weight training she did almost every day, Joyce had more time than ever to focus on her health. *She's one of* those *quarantining people...* Healthy food. Lots of exercise. Not like Abbie, who spent the first six weeks of lockdown stuffing her face with chips and binging Netflix, only going outside to walk Sammy by the beach. "These chats remain the highlight of my week."

"You're only saying that..."

"I'm serious. You've been keeping me sane this whole year. I talk to some of my friends online, and of course I have to Zoom with clients and coworkers, but it's not the same as leaning back in my underwear and having someone watch me orgasm all over the place."

"I mean... you didn't have to pick *me* for such an honor."

They both laughed. Abbie's phone informed her she was logged into the app. All she saw was a timer, a green Go button, and five "levels of intensity." "What the hell am I looking at?" Abbie asked.

"Why don't you push a button and find out?"

Abbie hated to admit it, but her curiosity got the best of her. She was so distracted by her app that she barely noticed that Joyce braced against her desk. Wasn't that what Abbie was always looking for during these sexy video chat dates? "I swear, if this is some crazy..."

She hit the middle button. Right away, Joyce slammed her hands against her desk, head thrown back and a cry of surprise ripping across the speakers.

"Whoa, whoa!" Panicking, Abbie held her phone in front of her. Although a part of her knew what she had done, she was in too much of a hurry to find the newly-red STOP button to dwell on the implications of her actions. "Hang on! I'm so sorry!"

She stopped the app. After a few seconds, Joyce let out a hoot of surprise and rubbed her hand down her face.

"Hot damn. That's some good shit," she said, "but you didn't have to stop."

"The hell I didn't! Did you see what happened to you?"

Still laughing, Joyce uprighted herself in her chair and pushed her hair out of her face. She already looked more relaxed than she had been a few minutes before. "As you can see, that's a very special power you've got in your hands."

"Is this to some fucking vibrator?" Abbie both loved it already and couldn't believe Joyce would be so *naughty!* "Do you have a vibrator up your pussy right this minute, Ms. Stewart?"

"You would too, if I had thought to send you one. Maybe for Christmas!"

"So..." Abbie beheld the power in her hand. "Is this what we're doing tonight? How long have you been waiting for me with that thing up your hoo-hah?"

Joyce shot her a diabolical look. "Less talking. Unless it's dirty talking, and your thumb is on that button."

Abbie could hardly believe her luck that year.

Chapter 2

"She is seriously something else." Abbie leaned back on the bench, the cool wind whipping against her face and the seagulls squawking overhead. The wind blew a little ocean spray her way, but she didn't mind. In fact, she found it refreshing. Why else would Abbie choose to live in Seaside, a place of swing sets on the sand and rollerblades tearing up the flat promenade separating the beach from the town. The bench was situated in front of a chain hotel that, somehow, convinced the off-season tourists to get in the damn swimming pool at that time of year. For Abbie, this was all a usual sight as someone who walked her dog and sat with a friend. "I don't wanna say I'm falling in love with someone I've yet to meet in the flesh, but whew."

The hearty chuckle on the other end of the phone line told her she had caught her dad in a good mood. Dwayne was always in a good mood, though. For a man who had rode the Dot Com Boom and now owned a couple properties around the state – and send all three of his kids to college – he had a lot to smile about. Even more so when it came to his only daughter, who had not-so-secretly been his favorite. *Don't feel bad for my brothers. They are total mama's boys.* Both of them. That's how twins worked.

"I'm happy for you, kiddo!" Although the wind fluttered and the ocean tumbled, Abbie could still clearly hear her father hundreds of miles away in Eugene. Taking such a shit year and spinning it into gold. Maybe you should meet this lady of yours soon. She lives in Portland, right? Sounds like a great chance for you to see each other on a weekend. Why haven't you yet?"

"Pandemic, Dad." Abbie's attention was caught by her dog's snout rooting for something in the grass behind them. Two seconds later, Sammy triumphantly sat back with someone's old tennis ball in her mouth. "She's been working at home since March, but I haven't. With the way case numbers have been lately, we haven't wanted to risk it."

"Uh huh, uh huh. Well! Sounds like something you should take care of soon enough. What's the point of having a house on the beach if you can't have your lady friend over sometime? It's been bad enough we haven't had much chance to visit this past summer. Of course, it if were up to me, I'd have spent all of August on the beach and in my fish and chips spot. But nooo, your mother insisted that we stay in Lane County. Kept telling her that Lane County includes Florence, but she wasn't having it."

Abbie ignored that part of her father's rant. "You're honestly not missing much here right now. The weather's been dunking on us, and there are still enough tourists around that you're not even getting away from it all. Only reason I'm out here is because the dog needs walking."

"Maybe you should get back inside for a couple weeks. Convince your lady friend to come for a visit. Eh? *Eh?*"

"Dad." Sometimes, it wasn't necessarily a good thing to have a dad who was so "supportive" of his daughter's sexuality. "Chill."

"Can't blame me for wanting you to bring someone home for Christmas for once. Hey, on that note, your mom wants to know if she should bother with the green bean casserole this year. You're the only one who really likes it."

Abbie had been dreading this. The part where her father slyly asked if she were coming home for Christmas that year. *That's why he's asking about the green bean casserole.* It was true that she loved her mother's Christmas fare. To the point she had considered taking two weeks off for Christmas to quarantine and head home. Except the more the season progressed, and the more life tore her in different directions, the less planning she had. Abbie had spent many nights and hours of downtime at work deciding what to do with her holidays. Her conclusion?

Nobody was going to like it.

"I don't think she needs to make green bean casserole this year." Abbie caressed the top of Sammy's head when she said that. Those happy eyes and flicking tongue only soothed her for a short second. Because another second later? Her dad sighed.

"Abbie..."

"I'm sorry, Dad."

"This would be the first Christmas we weren't all together since you did study abroad."

"I know. I know... I'm sorry, Dad. It's only at this point I don't think I can quarantine long enough to make sure I don't get anyone sick on accident. Ever since Mom had her surgery last year, I've wanted to be extra careful. It's one thing when Troy and Tony already live in Eugene and are in your bubble. Besides, you'll get to see your grandkids, right? Maybe you can

Zoom me in for dinner and opening presents. You might have to mail me my presents, by the way. If you do it now, I could get them by Christmas." That reminded Abbie she should probably return the favor. She had set aside a few gifts from the shop that her mother and nieces and nephews would love.

Dwayne was quiet. Quiet enough for Abbie to stare out at the ocean. Only then did she realize that nobody else was around. Nobody on the beach. Nobody jogging up the promenade in the rain. No dogs, except for Sammy. Perhaps one tourist sitting on a deck and watching the waves roll in. A car slowly turned in the roundabout by the beach, but that was it. Abbie was alone in a place that was usually packed with bodies on any other given year.

Moments like those allowed the loneliness to sink in.

"You gotta do what you gotta do, kiddo." Nevertheless, Dwayne sighed when he said that. "I had a feeling you might say that, but your mother's already in denial. It would mean a lot to her if the whole family was together for

Christmas this year, especially since we didn't have Thanksgiving. Your mom's taking this year *really* hard."

"I know, Daddy." Abbie's mother had to have ovarian cancer surgery over a year ago. *She missed out on the holidays because she was in recovery and couldn't be around people when she's already immunocompromised.* The deal was they would spend 2020 going on vacations, having holiday blowouts, and never missing a moment of the grandkids' school activities. Instead, some asshole virus had blown across the world and shuttered the whole Greywood family. Every time Abbie had a video chat with her mother, Sasha managed to keep it together until the moment her daughter was about to log off. Then the tears began. "Except I don't wanna accidentally get you or mom sick. I know everyone's made sacrifices this year." Tony's wife had taken a year-long leave of absence from her job so she could not only keep her kids home for school, but Troy's kids, too. *That woman is homeschooling three kids full time. I can't even imagine.* The Greywoods were lucky enough that their financial comfort allowed them to have bigger houses on the outskirts of Eugene, meaning they could quarantine in a bubble with relative ease. Except that left out youngest child Abbie, who had been leaving in Seaside for two years and was reticent to move back to Eugene for lockdown. While she would have been with her family, she would have missed the beach. Her privacy and independence. The life that continued to go on in touristy seafront communities – because the Portlanders didn't stop visiting because of some little virus.

Abbie had lots of conflicting thoughts and opinions on that, of course, but at the end of the day she decided to focus on what was within *her* control, and not everyone else's.

This? Being alone for Christmas while walking Sammy on the rainy beach? That was within her control. *Besides, everyone continuing to come visit this town means I really can't risk it.* That was the deduction she made every time she sat down for a self-risk assessment. One could never be too sure if they were asymptomatic, and getting tested without any symptoms had become... complicated... once again.

"You're a smart girl, Abs." Dwayne said that, yet she could hear the slight wibble in his voice. "We didn't raise an idiot. We'll see you again soon. Count on it. Time is gonna keep on flying like it always does."

"I can't wait for you guys to come back to the beach house, Dad. The summer wasn't the same without everyone stuffing themselves into a two-bedroom house." Kids on the couches and spouses trying to be quiet in the kitchen. Having the whole house to herself for so long almost lulled Abbie into thinking it was truly her place to do with as she pleased. In a way, that was true. Since the house got a lot of foot traffic, she upped the curb appeal that summer by replacing the sod and planting some azaleas by the fence. Most of them made it so far. *So far...* Winter was only getting colder. Here was hoping.

"I hope you can find some way to enjoy Christmas with someone, Abs. Seriously. Think about asking your lady friend to come stay with you. I won't even tell your mother so she won't get jealous. Or weirded out you have a girlfriend staying in a room we sleep in when we're there! You know she wants to pretend you're eighteen forever."

Abbie rolled her eyes. "If she finds out, tell her they're sleeping in the other bedroom." Before Covid, Abbie had kept the second bedroom as "off limits" to herself, so it was already prepared for someone in the family to drop by for a short visit. Since nobody had visited since February, though, more of Abbie's stuff had crept in there. She hung up a few posters that were collecting dust in the closet. That's where she stuck Sammy when the UPS guy drove up and she went a little nuts. The bed was still functional. She supposed that was all that mattered.

"We'll be celebrating Christmas together next year, Dad. Tell Mom I love her, and will try to set up a video chat with her sometime soon."

"You better. I'll break the news to her, but next time she sees you, she'll want to know exactly what kind and how many cookies she's sending you."

Abbie hung up a minute later. After pocketing her phone and gazing out at the gray ocean, she rubbed the top of Sammy's dewy head and asked her if they should stop by the pet store before heading home. Abbie wasn't in a hurry to go back to the house. She had to sort out a few things. Like how she might go about suggesting to Joyce that they finally meet up in a couple of weeks.

Sounds silly thinking about it at all. Of course Joyce wouldn't agree to it. She hadn't agreed to any of Abbie's other hints that they meet up over the summer. Why would she now?

Abbie needed to get used to the idea of Christmas by herself, for the first time ever. Perhaps that was one of the final frontiers of accepting she was finally an adult at the ripe young age of twenty-seven.

Chapter 3

Joyce always started her days with some kind of exercise. Running. Strength training. A walk through the woods or, as she was fond of while it was raining outside...

Yoga. Lots and lots of yoga.

There wasn't much space in her cramped one-bedroom apartment for exercise, but yoga was compact enough, as long as she moved her coffee table and was careful to not put the mat *too* close to the wall. She had a healthy list of yoga YouTubers she queued up before sitting legs crossed on the mat, breathing deeply and attempting to detach herself from the world.

Today, she squared her shoulders and pointed her nose toward the ceiling. Her baby pink sports bra strained against her chest, and the matching pants rustled against the mat. The timer on the TV continued to tick down until it was time to move into downward facing dog. As someone who spent her whole days on the computer, it was vital that Joyce stretch as much as she could before sitting down to do anything. *Check email. Study my bank account. Consider my future.*

Get lost down the YouTube black hole. Pick up a video game. Flip through a book. Play in Photoshop instead of doing her actual graphic design work. Whatever it took to take her mind off literally *everything*.

Her phone rang. She let it go to voicemail. Didn't bother to check to see who was calling.

Breathe in. Breathe out. It's a new day. Her corner of Portland was always eerily silent late Sunday mornings. Not even the church crowds were at it anymore. Occasionally, a small group of siblings took to the park across the street and played basketball, the dribbling ball and shouts of encouragement serenading Joyce when she had her window open during the summer.

Then she was serenaded by sirens. Banging pots and pans. Chanting for justice. Portland was now loud in all the wrong ways.

I need to move. She allowed her thoughts to be invaded by that, all the good it did her. *Can't afford to live here if I can't actually go out and do things. Or if I'm gonna be reminded of everything that makes me anxious.*

When she finished her yoga practice half an hour later, she sat back down on her mat and picked up her phone. The voicemail had been from her estranged aunt. Someone Joyce hadn't spoken to since February, the last time she visited home and said goodbye to an old life.

She knew what was on this message. After a deep breath, Joyce held the phone up to her ear and pressed play.

"Uh, hi Joyce... um..." her aunt began. *"So, uh, was calling to let you know that, um... well, your mom passed away last night. Ah... call me later if you have a chance. Hope you're doing well and staying safe. Bye."*

Joyce clicked her phone off and laid it beside her. She bent forward, the soles of her feet pressing together as she squeezed her toes and attempted to introduce her forehead to her lap. Her range of motion was never great. No matter how much she ran or stretched, the older Joyce got, the harder it was to do the things she used to take for granted in her early twenties.

Wasn't that how it went?

"Man..." She stretched her head back, then forward. Around in little circles. Once again, she bent forward, hoping this time she could stretch a little farther. Just a *little*.

I'm never gonna see my mom again.

Joyce had made peace with her mother's illness years ago. The woman had been diagnosed with dementia before Joyce even had the chance to move out on her home. Five years ago, her mother was moved into a nursing home. One year ago, she completely forgot who Joyce was when she came to visit. To say that Joyce was upset... well, of course she was. Yet she had cried those tears years ago. She had already lost so much. Her mother had been emotionally and mentally dead to her since the question, *"What do you want for Christmas, sweetheart? How about a doll?"* became the only thing her mother knew how to ask.

Eventually, though, she would have to call her aunt back. Find out what was happening on the funeral front. If there even was one. Covid had ensured nobody got to mourn properly or attend a damn burial with friends and family. One of Joyce's online coworkers lost his father at the start of the lockdowns and said the funeral was "him and a couple of people standing six feet apart." How were people supposed to grieve and move on from that?

Better for there to be no funeral. Joyce hoped that her mother's body was treated with respect. It was the least she deserved after sixty-nine years. *She had a hard life.* Sometimes, Joyce expressed her mother's troubles in her digital art. *In my off time, of course. Clients don't pay for that.* Clients paid for Facebook ad graphics, website headers, and calling cards to shove into newsletters. Joyce was damn good at what she did and charged accordingly, but it didn't allow her to express what she really felt in her lonely heart.

She dragged herself over to her desk and brought her computer out of sleep. One of her original creations, a woman grasping a handful of stars before being sucked into the void of a black hole, gaped back at her on the lock screen. Joyce stared at it before punching in her Windows pin and meeting the screens she forgot to close before going to bed the night before.

One of those was the video client she shared with Abbie, the highlight of her year.

They had met back in May, when one of the many online dating sites advertised rock-bottom rates for those looking for love online during quarantine. Joyce had signed up after a late night of drinking wine and blaring Swedish pop music while she dithered between drawing porn and reading smut she found online. Instead, she put up one of her better selfies and described herself as a "lesbian who draws good." The next day, she had been matched with Abbie, and the rest had felt like history.

Exchanging private messages. Texting. Video chatting. *Sometimes daily.* Hell, the cyber sexing had happened sooner than Joyce ever anticipated. *I guess it was organically...* One night they had been chatting on the phone, when Joyce made the offhand comment that she was in bed naked because it was too damn hot in Portland. Instead of merely suggesting she come over to the beach to cool off, Abbie had said something along the lines of, *"Wish I was there."*

Why shouldn't they have phone sex? Cyber? Get each other off over (encrypted) video chat? Joyce was definitely the type to hop into bed on the first date if the chemistry was there, and the chemistry had been sizzling from the first video chat that reaffirmed how adorable Abbie was with her dirty blond hair pulled back into messy ponytails and her sweaters falling off her shoulders. She was the exact kind of woman Joyce wanted to pounce upon in the sack, batteries sometimes included.

Part of the fun, of course, was the forbidden nature of them meeting up in real life. The virus ensured they stayed physically apart, and it gave Joyce something to look forward to every

Friday night, even if all she and Abbie did was lie in bed and stare at each other through a screen.

Usually they had some kind of sex, though. Usually. Highlight of Joyce's week. *I'm getting laid more now than I did in the before times, so that's something.* She was running more, too. Eating better now that the initial depression had passed. Honestly, she didn't have much of a social life before lockdown. Sure, she had her coping mechanisms that kept her from thinking about her mother's impending death or the fact she had few in real life friends, but that all felt like the past now.

Her fingers hovered over the keyboard. She was about to tell Abbie about the phone call when three bubbles appeared at the bottom of the screen.

Abbie was already typing something!

"Hey! You on? I know it's kinda early, but I really wanna talk."

Joyce pulled herself back with a start. Chat? Now? Why, she hadn't showered yet! Or ate lunch! Did she look a mess? Would Abbie hear her stomach growling through the speakers? Joyce grabbed her flab as it flopped out of her yoga pants. "You behave, okay?" While Abbie had seen her naked plenty of times before, it was always in context. Lingerie. Totally nude. A hot dress that slit up the side and made her tits – the true focal point of her body! – hang out. She was mighty shy about her belly flab, though. She supposed it couldn't be helped.

Her stray hairs and her lack of makeup could be, though. Well, she wouldn't bother putting on makeup for a non-sexy date with Abbie, but she would double-check her hair.

Two minutes later, Abbie was on the screen, wearing a baggy black sweatshirt and sitting on her couch with the dog wagging its tail beside her.

"Heeey! Hope I'm not interrupting your workout!" Abbie's camera lagged whenever she waved. The dog kept its eyes on those moving hands. "This is really sudden, I know, but I wanted to talk to you about something."

While this was a welcomed distraction from the news she had received, Joyce couldn't help but think about the voicemail on her phone. *I was about to tell her that my mom finally died.* Abbie knew the whole saga with the dementia and how it had affected Joyce's grieving process over the years, but she would be the first to hear from Joyce that things had finally come to their natural end. *Or I could wait until later, I guess.* Wasn't like it tore Joyce's heart in two or came out of nowhere. Ashes to ashes. Dust to dust. *And all that.*

Besides, she didn't want to be a total Debbie Downer. Not when Abbie had that big smile on her face and a happy dog beside her.

"Oh, it's fine," Joyce squeaked, before clearing her throat. "I finished my yoga. Was about to go take a shower and have lunch, but I can wait a bit."

"Ooh, a shower? You're gonna be naked, huh?"

Joyce giggled. "As naked as I usually am when we chat."

"Yeah, but you're in your cute pink yoga outfit. Imagine if I was there to take full advantage of your downward facing dog."

"I admit, I sometimes have the thought when I linger in the position..." Couldn't be helped. When Joyce was horny and doing yoga, she thought about sex when her ass was up in the air and her legs slightly apart. *What? I never promised to be a super-mature adult.* Everything she learned, she learned from her mother, one of the dirtiest minds on the planet until it all went to hell. "Anyway, I'm not going to be naked until you tell me what's on your mind. So? What's up?"

Abbie clapped her hands together in anticipation. Sammy the border collie barked her enthusiasm, as if they were about to introduce the brand-new fridge Joyce had won on "The Price is Right." "I had to tell my dad yesterday that I won't be making it home for Christmas. Let me tell you, that wasn't an easy decision to make."

"You're... excited about that?"

"What? Oh, no. I'm excited about what I thought about doing instead. Actually, it was my dad's idea. He's really worried about me being alone for this Christmas. It will actually be my first time being all by myself... even when I studied abroad, I had my super-Catholic host family in Costa Rica to celebrate with me and teach me their customs. So... um..."

"Yeah?"

"I was wondering if maybe you..." Abbie righted her posture and blinked so heavily that she looked like she was breaking out of a trance. "If maybe you would like to come visit me for Christmas."

It took a few seconds for those words to sink into Joyce's brain. "Huh?" Yet that was all she could say.

"Yeah. I had a feeling that might be your response. Except you miss every shot you don't take, right?" Abbie snapped her fingers. The dog was beside herself in excitement. "Right. So, I asked. You asked me *huh?* Now I know."

"I didn't say no..."

"So you're thinking about it? Come on, Joy, it's been like seven months, and we still haven't had any skin-to-skin contact." Abbie bit her lap as she pulled her laptop closer to her face. Soon, she was nothing but eyebrows and pores. "I'm going nuts here, man." Why did she lower her voice? Was there someone else in the house with her? "If I could have anything for Christmas, it would be your pussy in my face."

Joyce couldn't help but snort in mild amusement. "You keep building up my pussy like it's going to blow your mind. I dunno what else to do for you. You've seen it like a hundred times now. I even sent you close-up Polaroids." Some of that same wine from the time she put herself "out there" helped her have the courage to mail dirty pictures of herself to someone on the Oregon coast. *Where are my pictures, huh?* That's what Joyce wanted to say now, to mess with Abbie, who got gigglier than a kid at The Enchanted Forest during summer vacation.

"There's nothing to build up when I know it's going to be great." Abbie puffed out her cheeks. Suddenly, the dog's face was there, too. Abbie pushed her away and continued. "How could it not be great?"

"That's a lot of pressure on my vagina."

Abbie frowned. "You called it your vagina on purpose, didn't you?"

"Aw, did my clinical use of the correct term kill your lady boner?"

"On a Sunday morning, no less."

Joyce checked the time on her computer. "Barely morning. It's eleven-fifty."

"Hey, hey. You haven't answered the question yet. About coming to visit for Christmas."

Sighing, Joyce's whole body sagged into her chair. "What do you want me to say? The only reason we haven't actually met up is because of the fucking coronavirus. Like..." She held up her hands, as if to say, *"What do you want from me?"*

"Do you at least want to? Even if you can't?"

That hit Joyce right in the chest, as if someone had climbed over her computer monitor and laid a punch right into her ribcage. *Hard enough to knock me back in my chair.* She even placed her hand over her heart. Would she be surprised if she bruised later? No. Hardly anything surprised her anymore.

"Of course I want to visit," Joyce softly said. "I've wanted to come visit you at the beach ever since we started fooling around over chat. It's killing me that I can't give you a kiss even after everything we've done so far. I mean, I've told you some of my more traumatic secrets." Not only her mother. Toxic exes. Losing her childhood home. That time in college when she tried to end it all. Joyce was probably too much of an open book with someone she had yet to touch with her bare hand. "Summer at the beach would have been beautiful. The photos you post on social media got me jealous."

Abbie finally pulled away from her camera. "Yeah. Drives me nuts I've got this great girl on the computer, but I can't even be seen with her around here. I know the perfect time to go to the surf when nobody else is around. I wanna buy you gelato. Chocolate dipped waffle cones."

"Sounds heavenly."

"It is! Instead of mailing you taffy, how about we share one, huh? I'll finally have a reason to put up some decorations. Like I said, this will be my first Christmas without anyone."

I've spent more than a few alone. Abbie didn't want to hear that, though. Nor did she want to hear how much Joyce actually detested Christmas. If the commercialism wasn't bad enough? *The memories. They hurt too much.*

"How about I'll think about it?" That was the closest Joyce would get to agreeing today. "I'd have to figure things out, you know. I mean, I've got time off around Christmas, anyway, but it's not like you've been quarantining this whole time."

"Yeah... bit late for me to take time off right now. I admit, you'd be putting yourself at some risk for me."

"Not like I have anyone I worry about exposing..."

"Hm? Are you talking yourself into it?"

Joyce chuckled. "I want to come visit, Abs. Even though I'll probably be on my period and won't want anyone touching me. Not even Cate Blanchett." She knew that would get the point across. Sometimes, they spent their Friday night dates streaming movies together. *Carol* had been one of their mutual favorites, back when they did a Christmas in July film fest for a whole weekend. *I was on my period. Go figure.*

So much take-out ordered. So many candid chats while soaking in the bath. It was like they were never apart, not even when they slept. *She watched me go to sleep. I'll never forget it.*

Like she would never forget the day she realized she was truly falling for Abbie, a twenty-something only two hours away. Two far, lonely hours that Joyce couldn't agree to bridge while the world was on fire. Sometimes, literally.

They hadn't exchanged the L word yet. It didn't feel right. Not with their relationship completely online.

"Guess you could say it's my one Christmas wish," Abbie said. "The one wish that could actually come true. Don't think I could completely rid my mom of cancer forever or halt a freakin' pandemic. But seeing you. Kissing you..." She turned the camera away before she started blushing. "I like to think that's within our control... but I won't ask you to do anything you're not comfortable with. Don't think I want to put our relationship on the rocks like that. It's not only about me and what I want. I mean... what do *you* want for Christmas?"

Joyce couldn't put to words what was running through her head. *To pretend Christmas doesn't exist? To have my mom back? To be a little girl and waking up on Christmas morning, smelling my mom's French toast and hearing her tell me to get up so I can open presents?* Joyce had few of her mother's presents left. Most of them were gone. Donated. Lost. Forgotten.

She pretended to drop something on the floor so she had an excuse to bend down and wipe something from her eye. *Don't do it now. Save the crying for later. She doesn't need that.*

"I guess finally getting to share a bed with you would be a nice way to spend Christmas." Joyce sat back up, confident that she wouldn't start crying anytime soon. *Distract me, Abs, but not with thoughts of the holidays.* "I know it's rainy and cold and shit, but walking on the beach and maybe throwing a stick for your dog would be rad. Pancakes. Make me pancakes, and we'll talk about my next risk assessment."

"Uh, I'm not a great cook. You know that, right? Tell you what. I'll take you out to the Pig 'n' Pancake. Way better than what I... right. You don't want to risk going to restaurants."

"Man, I haven't been to a restaurant in months. Unless I was picking up takeout." More than once Joyce thought about doing patio service when the weather was nice, but by herself? She didn't want all those eyes on her. It would be different from "the before times," when nobody paid any mind to who sat next to them in a cozy restaurant. Now? A part of her was afraid to be judged. Silly, wasn't it? *Doesn't take much, I'm afraid.* "Stop selling this so well! Maybe I like being a total shut-in who doesn't remember what the sunrise looks like!"

"I can't sell you a sunrise on the beach since, you know, geography." Abbie rubbed her dog's ear. "But I can sell you a sunset on the beach. I've seen a hundred of them, and they never stop being gorgeous. Even in shit weather like we have right now. Hey, bring your hoodies, all right? Although I've got a ton you can borrow from me."

"Now I'm borrowing your hoodies? We really are girlfriends, aren't we?"

Abbie's chuckles transformed into a hearty laugh. "Why wouldn't we be, hon?"

While a war of thoughts waged within Joyce, she focused on her purple computer mouse, which lit up every time she moved it around a little. *Purple was my mother's favorite color...* The only saving grace about the holidays was that purple never played a big part in the decorating and festivities. For the best. When young Joyce ran out of options for her mother, she always defaulted to something pleasantly purple. *You'd think my old house had burned down, from how little I still have.* Her mother once told her a story of her very first husband, a man who defaulted on their storage shed and lost everything she had from her childhood. Joyce's mother had always begged her to never let something like that happen again.

And yet...

"You okay?"

Joyce looked up and met Abbie's pretty face. Those soft brown eyes and those freckles by the lips always made Joyce smile – even when her thoughts were dominated by memories she would never get to relive again.

"I'm fine. Just a lot to think about, isn't it?"

"If I come up with a plan that makes it great for both of us, trust me, I'll let you know. Oh, and..." Abbie moved her laptop to the coffee table. Instantly, Sammy the dog appeared in the camera, panting and grinning. "Let me know if you might be bringing your Aunt Flo with you. I can plan around that too, you know."

"I was joking about that!"

"Either way..." Sammy's ears flopped up in the air as Abbie gave her a face rub. "Let me know, huh? Don't feel pressured to do anything. We could also spend Christmas like we've spent every video date since late May."

"Suppose it would be around the anniversary of our first video chat," Joyce said.

"Yup! Hey, so, no matter what we both decide, it's going to be a date on Christmas. I'll wear my sexiest ugly sweater if you wear yours."

The smile slightly faltered on Joyce's face. "I don't have one."

"What! That won't do. I'll either have to get you one myself, or have my mom send me one of her many, *many* spares. It's sort of a thing back in my house. I'm gonna miss it this year."

"Your family does the ugly Christmas sweater thing?"

"Are you shocked? Everything I've told you about my family this year has made it sound like they come straight out of some corny comedy movie about meeting the crazy in-laws."

"They don't sound like that..."

"Let me have it, huh?" Abbie finished petting her dog and enticed Sammy to walk away with a big, hearty thump to the rump. "Next time we talk, you can tell me all about Christmas with your family. With our powers combined..."

Joyce stopped listening there. She was too busy contorting her face to make it look like she was paying attention, instead of doing what she desperately avoided.

Crying.

Chapter 4

Things were not going well in Casa de Greywood. Mostly because Abbie had no idea what she was doing, and every time she attempted to "fake it 'til she made it," embarrassment overcame her in ways that should not have rattled a confident women in her late twenties.

Part of the problem was Sammy. Every time Abbie started getting a little comfortable, her dog was either shoving her snout beneath the door or whining against the knob. *I thought I gave you a good walk earlier!* Plenty good walk to knock Sammy out for a few hours while Abbie took *care* of some things.

Like putting together a sexy care package for her girlfriend, who had been so kind to send one her way a week ago!

Abbie had thought about it all day at work. While locals came in to do some Christmas shopping for their loved ones in other parts of the country, Abbie stood behind the front counter, hornier than ever. *So. Embarrassing.* Nothing like distracting herself by spritzing down the jewelry case while an octogenarian asked her opinion on birthstone jewelry that Abbie knew nothing about.

What do these people want from me, anyway? She restocked shelves, rang up orders, and cleaned up when she was done! That was it! Sid was the one whose whole family was a bunch of new-age, crystal-using hippies. Although, if she were being honest, her family wasn't too far off from that, either.

The only answer to her conundrum was to go straight home at five, walk the dog, feed them both, and change into something more comfortable. Like a choice piece of lingerie that arrived in the mail the day before.

"Fuck me, I know not what I'm doing." Abbie had tried everything, from putting up her hair to propping her phone against her desk. Yet every time she tried to take a photo, she was overcome with the sillies. Her! Abbie Greywood! The woman who wasn't afraid to tell Joyce, *"I wish I was there with you right now,"* when she announced that one was naked beneath the covers. Taking sexy pictures of herself, let alone the kind Joyce had taken for her? Impossible.

Maybe Abbie's problem was that she wasn't used to being sexy by herself. Masturbating? Fine. Job done. Having sex, even if over a webcam? Sure! Why not? When the focus could be on either her fantasies or someone else, everything was fine. Easy. No better way to go crazy!

Except taking sexy photos of herself meant she was alone. Focusing on herself. No fantasies, only the *what ifs* that plague the mind when left to its own devices.

Abbie checked herself in the mirror again. One of her breasts was threatening to pop out of her Christmas-green lingerie, and not in the fun way. *Nothing sexy about a boob that has its own agenda.* Abbie shoved it back into place and straightened out the lacy skirt around her thighs. All she could do was compare them to Joyce's. *She fills out everything so nicely. You can tell she goes running every day...* Joyce's thighs were on the thicker side, but that only made them sexier when she wore her lingerie for their dates. How many times had she wished she could shove her face between Joyce's legs and die happy?

I don't know how to be sexy without someone else here with me. The eternal conundrum.

Abbie propped her phone up on her headboard. She had the camera set to fire off a series of photos while she sat up on her knees and bunched her hair on top of her head. *Is this sexy?* Should she pout? Coyly tug on her lingerie? Cheekily stick out her butt and wiggle it a little? *What is the line between sexy nudes and pornography?* The sad thing? Abbie was no stranger to nudes. Like a true, young idiot, she had sent plenty to her girlfriends and people online when she was in college. So what happened? Did the full brain development mean she saw the shame in doing such naughty deeds? Or was it different because this was Joyce, a woman who was so effortlessly sexy that Abbie still couldn't believe they were fooling around over a webcam several months later?

Would we even be going out if we met in real life?

It was an unfortunate thought she had every time she stopped and considered about it too long. Joyce was a successful city woman who oozed beauty. She was only four years older than Abbie, but already seemed to have her whole life together. When she talked about the "before times" of running groups, trash collecting meetups, and bar nights with buddies in her industry, Abbie had to conceal her jealousy. *Price you pay if you choose to live on the beach instead of the city, I guess.* Sometimes, Abbie wanted to say screw it and move to Portland. Except she could never afford it, even if her parents had a vacation home there. Not like Joyce, who was a professional graphic designer who did massive gigs for marketing companies and the clients themselves. How could Abbie ever compare herself to *that?*

She looked like an utter fool trying to pose sexy on her bed. If she was committed to turning Joyce on with surprise nudes, she had to... well, *commit.* Posing in lingerie wasn't going to cut it. She had rip off some of her clothes and turn on the vibrator. Kinda like Joyce had in some of her photos.

If only Abbie could get away with framing those and putting them on her nightstand...

She grabbed a glass dildo from the drawer and held it up to her pursed lips. *So. Silly.* Yet she committed, because that's what she came into this room to do. Her dog wasn't pacing up and down the hallway for nothing! Nor was Joyce probably in the shower right now, not knowing what she was about to receive, for nothing. Abbie had told Sid she couldn't hang out that night. She had also foregone a phone call back home to her family so she could do this. *This!*

Whatever this was, honestly.

All right. You know what she wants. Tease her with the O face, girl.

Abbie looked between what was in her hand and what was between her thighs. For some reason, the two would not meet.

Oh, God. Oh, no. This is gonna end up in the cloud, isn't it? Fuck me. Someone's gonna hack this. They're gonna find pictures of me with a glass dildo up my pussy and my bunched-up monster face on the other end. Fuck me. Oh, no. What do I do?

She inhaled a deep breath. Slowly, the glass dildo made its way down her chest, Abbie's eyes squeezed shut and her thighs refused to part.

Someone chose that exact moment to call her.

Of course, the phone blaring a loud-ass tone at her snapped Abbie right out of any fantasy she was about to concoct to get her through this embarrassing photo session. After yelping into the crook of her arm, Abbie shoved the dildo under her pillow, as if whoever was calling her would see it through the phone.

It was Joyce. The one person Abbie didn't mind seeing her in a compromising position.

"Heeey." Abbie collapsed onto the bed, phone to her ear. "Wasn't expecting to hear you calling tonight. You'll never guess what I..."

"Hi."

Abbie refrained from finishing her riveting thought about sex and cameras. "What's up? You okay?" While Joyce wasn't a bastion of positive energy, she didn't usually sound *this* down. Let alone when calling Abbie out of thin air. "You sound a little different." *Oh, no. Is she sick?* A year ago, that would have been enough to make Abbie sad, especially if it affected Joyce coming to visit for Christmas. This year, though? The thought of anyone being sick instantly struck panic into her heart.

"Sorry. It's been a long day." Joyce cleared her throat. Only then did she sound a little more like her old self. "I had to work all day, and the weather was too crappy for me to go for a walk or a run. It's that time of year, you know.

As soon as I get up, the sun is already going down. Can't go out and meet up with people. Just sitting here in my apartment, trying to tell myself that yoga is the answer to everything."

Abbie didn't know what to say for a minute. While it wasn't unusual for Joyce to have a bad day – and Abbie couldn't blame her, since the woman lived in a tiny apartment in a city where everything bad that could have happened *did* – she didn't usually call up to vent. "Anything I can do to help?"

"Wanted to hear your voice, I guess. The Christmas stuff going up around here is starting to get to me. Everyone's pretending everything is normal this year, even though it isn't. Makes me wish I was anywhere else."

"You know..." Abbie bit her lip. "My invitation is still open. Tell me what day you want to come, and I'll have the guest room ready for you."

"Guest room? You mean I wouldn't be making a tent in your own bed with you every night? Telling ghost stories before we get to fooling around?"

"I mean... is that what you want?" Abbie asked.

Joyce sighed. "Yes. God, yes."

Although that wasn't Joyce confirming she'd be heading straight to Seaside the next day, it made Abbie relax for the first time since she got home.

***

One had to be careful going out for a run after a big, fresh rain. When the maple trees lost their coverage in late fall, every sidewalk, gutter, and outdoor patio was covered in the festive browns and beiges that made up Portland's enigmatic maples.

But damn if they weren't slippery little shits after the rain!

"Whoa!" That was the sound of a man going down on the sidewalk about ten yards away from Joyce, who slowed down when she came upon him and the mess of maple leaves flying off the concrete. She asked him if he was all right. He pulled up the bandana that covered his face and shook her off, claiming, "That's like the second time it's happened this week. You'd think I've learned." Without another word, he took off running as if nothing had happened.

Forget snow. It's these leaves you have to worry about. Joyce had to stop and catch her breath before taking off again. The earbuds in her ears pumped through a podcast about global warming and all the ways the earth was doomed to die. Instead of subjecting herself to more of that, she swapped over to a symphonic metal album that did wonders to drown out her thoughts. The only downside was it made her forget to check on her surroundings as she entered the wooded trails separating urban Portland from the forests beyond.

If she thought maple leaves on the sidewalk were dangerous...

I don't care. Of course she cared, a little. Yet that's what the expensive health insurance was for. Wouldn't be the first time Joyce tripped and sprained her ankle. Probably wasn't the last time, either. *I don't care.* Pain meant she was still alive. Having something tangible to worry about meant her brain worked. *Everything is relative. I don't care.* Her mother was dead after a long battle with dementia. Her aunt said she was taking care of everything, but there would be no funeral for now. Did that mean Joyce's mother would be buried in the plot purchased for her years ago? How was that working?

Just an unceremonious departure into the earth? Nobody around to care? *Fuck COVID. Fuck 2020. Fuck all of this.*

She ran harder and faster than she had in a while. Maybe it was the blue, partly-cloudy sky that made her feel like she could run and never stop. Just keep going. Feet flying across paved paths and cultured trails that could slide into the creeks at any time – only needed one big rain to slide it all into oblivion. Kicking through wild mushrooms and encountering glistening spiderwebs as she took a path nobody else had that day. Whenever the sun parted through the evergreen trees and hit her face, Joyce shielded her eyes and imagined what it would be like to keep running until she took off into the sky.

My mother's dead. I don't talk to my aunt. I have no other family. Her father had died in surgery two years ago. Not that she had a relationship with him. *I felt nothing when my aunt called and told me. Absolutely nothing.* Likewise, she had felt nothing when she found out her mother had died. Any grief that still lingered in her system had come from years and years ago – those long, lonely nights when she cried into her pillow because she "wanted her mommy."

Mommy had left the planet several years ago. Death was a formality. Funerals were unnecessary for a woman who had little friends, anyway. Yet, in a way, not having a funeral meant that the suspension continued in Joyce's heart. She hadn't properly said goodbye yet.

The worst part? Two weeks before that fateful phone call, she had the sudden urge to call her mother's memory care facility. Yet what had been the point? Joyce had stopped calling a long time ago. Every time she had, her mother instantly put down the phone and wandered away, only for a nurse to eventually pick up and say, "Guess she was done, huh?" Visiting her the few times Joyce had the chance also only proved to be worse than it was worth. Joyce and her aunt had stopped visiting because it upset Joyce's mother way too much. *We were the only people the memory care facility told to stop visiting!* Why make her mother so upset with a simple hello?

So here Joyce was. Running through the forest, trying to feel alive for a while longer.

She flew out of the woods much sooner than she anticipated. Either that, or her mind had been so preoccupied that she didn't realize how fast she ran – or how quickly time went by. For one moment she was pushing away thoughts of her mother, and the next?

Back on her street, heading toward her apartment building.

The seasons had changed without any regard for the real world that year. Now, a little later than usual, people were outside hanging up Christmas lights and deciding at the last minute to host mini-parades for the kids who had already missed out on Halloween. The inflatable Santas waved back at her. Glowing reindeer flashed by fence posts. Someone sat out on their apartment balcony, blasting Christmas songs. The wreaths the city had hung up on light posts fluttered in the wind. Advertisements asking people to please be careful that winter as cases continued to rise only served to remind everyone that nothing was normal. This was a year when Joyce walked by playgrounds and cringed at how many kids trampled upon structures.

Nothing was normal. Everything felt weird and wrong. Her only chance at normalcy was going back into her shell of an apartment and listening to music while she worked.

She stopped to check her mail before heading up the stairs to her apartment. *No elevator today. Gotta stay in shape.* That was barely enough for her to stay sane. Used to be, she walked everywhere. Meetups? Walk. Grocery trips? Walk. Dates?

Usually, she walked.

Now, she drove everywhere, if she went somewhere at all. Groceries were delivered to her door. All of her meetups were online. Dates?

She thought of Abbie, who had patiently listened to her last night.

Joyce hadn't told her what happened with Mom. There was no point dragging that up. Nor was it a matter of, *"If I admit to it, then it's true, and I can't have that."* Joyce was painfully aware how "real" it was. Maybe that was why she didn't want to talk about. *If I bring it up, then that's all we talk about. Even if I want to change subjects, it's a, "I'm here for you, okay?"* It wasn't anyone's fault. For most decent people, that was the inclination. People wanted to show sympathy. Be there for someone who had suffered a loss. Community. Family.

Those words sounded so weird that year.

Unlike Abbie, Joyce had no pets. Not even a cat, although she thought about getting a kitten that year. Except her apartment was so small, and she was often so busy, that she worried a kitten wouldn't be fine in such a situation. Better to not have to take care of a small creature. She could barely take care of herself.

Even so, she still felt that emptiness when she opened her door and dumped her few items on her desk. She kicked off her running shoes and turned them upside down to dry on the windowsill. She had forgotten to turn off the TV before she left, so an illuminated screen blinded her when she looked in the wrong direction. After Joyce turned it off, she went into her bedroom and peeled off her running gear. A shower would do nicely between lunch and afternoon work.

A message awaited her on her phone. It was from Abbie.

Not the usual "good morning" texts, though. Hell. No.

What the shit? Nothing but a long set of pictures, and Joyce wasn't sure what she was looking at in the first place. Abbie? In green lingerie? *When did she get that? I haven't seen it before.* Abbie making duck lips? Pouting? Sticking out her ass and pretending to smack it?

Was that a glass dildo?

"What. The." Joyce stood in her bathroom doorway, scrolling through the photos that continued to confound her. A note that said, *"Was thinking of you last night,"* both confused and titillated Joyce, who was soon staring at Abbie's pussy and the glass dildo. "Oh, my God."

These weren't merely nudes. It was actual porn.

Laughing, Joyce shut off her phone and tossed it onto her bed. She finished the trek to the shower, where she ran hot water from the faucet and kept laughing like that was the funniest shit.

It wasn't that Abbie trying to be sexy with her homemade, amateur porn was *stupid*. It was the fact that Joyce came home from her angsty run to *that!*

Maybe that day wasn't so bad, after all. Didn't Joyce have something to look forward to staring at when she came out of the shower now? Something to make her smile before she sat down to work on a client's billboard graphic that would soon appear on freeways in Arizona?

If only they knew what I was looking at while I Photoshop a branded drink into a middle-aged woman's hand. The truly funny thing? Joyce was far from the only one looking at inappropriate materials while working from home. Perhaps that was the one bonus to a shitty year that forced her to stay inside and eschew all in-person touch.

Perhaps, that could change soon.

Instead of going straight to her desk, Joyce picked up her phone again when she stepped out of the shower and responded to Abbie's dirty pictures.

"I want to come visit you this Christmas. How does next Wednesday sound?"

From the enthusiastic response she soon received, that sounded amazing.

Chapter 5

"For real, though." Abbie slit open the package with a box cutter. Packing peanuts immediately spilled out onto the glass counter she had cleaned. "What the hell do I suggest we do?" She pulled out the boxes of aptly titled "stocking stuffers" that would soon be in the front window of the shop. "There's the beach, of course." The thought of Joyce, in her fuzzy sweaters and wool hats having a blast on the swing sets, brought an instant smile to Abbie's face. "Maybe she'd be into some hiking if the weather is good enough, but I don't know how she'll feel about going out to eat. Nobody here has any decent patio service, and it's too damn cold, anyway."

"There's Mo's," Sid said, referring to a famous fish and chips place right on the beach. While it was true one could enjoy a decent sunset there on a clear day...

"Too cold." Abbie swept packing peanuts into an empty box. "We're talking about a woman who has been inside and getting her grocery's delivered since March. I'm honestly shocked she agreed to come."

Sid waggled his eyebrows. "From the sounds of things, you should take the whole week off and entertain her at home. Take her to the beach when the dog has to go, and do all your grocery shopping before she gets here." He picked up a pen and wrote something on the inventory sheet. "Hit up the Grocery Outlet for all of your bulk purchasing needs."

"Dollar General up in Gearhart is having some sort of sale right now..."

"Dollar General is good if you what you need is your non-perishable dry goods..." Sid shrugged. "Or decorations."

"Oh!" Abbie dropped the box on her foot, but it wasn't heavy enough to make her cry out in pain. "I have an excuse to decorate! Dude! I gotta get a Christmas tree!"

"Make sweet love to your lady before the roaring fireplace."

Abbie's eyes glazed over. "Please don't give me ideas. It's bad enough that I'm ovulating."

"Abs." Sid leaned against the counter. "There are some things a guy doesn't need to know. For example, you don't need to know why I take a bathroom break every afternoon."

"You make it sound like 'ovulating' is akin to the levels of fibers in my diet."

"All I know is that I hear *ovulating* and I want an omelet from the Pig 'n' Pancake."

The box of packing peanuts was soon in the corner, where Abbie could empty the box of inventory on the counter and toss the peanuts behind her without worrying about a huge mess. "Beach. Hiking."

"Dog walking."

He had her there. "We could ride the carousel, if she doesn't mind being inside..."

"Take her to the Candyman. She'll love the music selection in there."

"Walks up and down the promenade." Abbie leaned her elbows against the counter and sighed. "Holding hands. Dodging kids on bikes and people with unleashed dogs..."

Sid turned over the clipboard with the inventory and snorted. "You really paint a beautiful picture of this town. The council should hire you for their tourism board."

"Ugh. We're gonna need it once the vaccines roll out." She didn't have to expand further for him. While tourists still swarmed the beaches that summer, it wasn't in the same numbers they had in years past. *This keeps up, and one of us is gonna get axed.* It would probably be Abbie, because she couldn't lift some of the boxes Sid dealt with every day. Besides, he knew how to run the register in her absence, anyway. She was useless compared to him!

"That reminds me. Still gotta get my flu shot."

"Sid!"

"What? I didn't have insurance! You gonna pay forty bucks out of pocket for anything but a COVID vaccine right now?"

Abbie moved the box off the counter and lined up the goods they both had to get to work putting away. "If we had a vaccine right this moment, I wouldn't have to worry about Joyce coming to visit and freaking out. It's bad enough so many people around here won't wear their mask. She says in Portland proper it's almost 100% compliance. Can you believe it?"

She didn't understand why Sid was chuckling at her. Only a second later did Abbie realize she had been fidgeting with her own mask. *Ugh! Now I gotta change it, wash my hands, the works!* It had been nine months, and she still wasn't used to it.

"So, what should I get her for Christmas?" Right. Changing the subject it was!

"You mean besides your hot bod?"

"I'm serious, Sid. If she's going to be in my house on Christmas, I wanna get her something nice. Something I wouldn't usually send through the mail." There were already a couple gifts Abbie had in her online shopping carts that she was planning on having gift wrapped and sent straight to Joyce's. *Why do that when*

I could wrap them myself and watch her open them in person?

"Could always get her some jewelry from the antique shops."

"Isn't that a bit much? I mean, it's our first time meeting in person. We've only been dating for a few months!"

"I said *jewelry,* Abs, not a diamond ring."

Abbie couldn't help but blush. *The thought of being engaged to her...* No, that was ridiculous. Abbie would never broach such a thing until she was sure. Or until they had been together in person long enough to know that they were truly compatible. Otherwise, it wasn't enough. *God help me if I propose to someone over the internet!* Abbie didn't care how many times she saw those breasts or watched those eyes roll back. It wasn't the same as a real kiss.

"Could always take her to the aquarium!" Sid called as he went back into the rear room of the shop. "With our complete absence of actual tide pools around here! Have her pet a stingray!"

"You're not helping!" Abbie crossed her arms and leaned against the counter. *I want to do everything with her. Show her the best time of her year. It doesn't have to be all about sex...* Sure, that would be an amazing highlight, but spending time with Joyce meant so much more to Abbie, who was otherwise alone that Christmas.

And falling in love – but she had admitted that to herself long, long ago when Joyce looked at the camera *just* right with a girlish grin on her face.

I want her to fall in love with this place, and maybe with me... If Joyce wasn't already falling in love with Abbie. In which case... nah, Abbie didn't want to know.

She closed her eyes and focused on the muted Christmas music playing over the speakers. She could barely make out "Have Yourself a Merry Little Christmas." *Judy Garland. Meet Me in St. Louis.* One of Abbie's favorite movies when she was a little girl. *I watched it every year. Wore out the VHS tape and was the only teenager on the planet asking for the DVD for Christmas.* Her parents had hunted it down for her. Nobody understood her love for Judy's bodacious red hair or the colorful garments of the movie, but that didn't matter.

She wondered if Joyce would watch it with her. Sharing something Abbie loved so much with someone she was falling in love with... that was it. That was her whole reason for thinking about taking a week off to quarantine, if that's what Joyce asked of her.

Then again, Joyce could ask her to wade out into the Pacific Ocean and become one with the jellyfish and crustaceans. At that point, Abbie was a big enough fool to do it.

***

"Nobody's saying they don't *like* it, Joyce." The head of marketing for Portland Creative, a multimedia company that often contracted Joyce's services, was lagging a little while he communicated to her via Zoom. "It isn't only checking off the boxes. They have to roll this out to their social media campaigns this time next week. The last great marketing push to get people to buy, buy, buy. If the customers aren't feeling the holiday charge, then they're not going to buy."

Joyce hated that everyone she worked with now was a hipster. While she didn't *hate* hipsters, per se, she lived in Portland. After a while, they got on her nerves, especially the way they talked. *Always finding a way to sound super passive aggressive, because we don't have enough of that in this town.* "Honestly not sure what you're trying to say, Will." Joyce attempted to keep a straight face instead of showing him the glower that haunted her emotions. "I followed all of the instructions. Matched the color palette they provided and everything." That hadn't been easy. The company had asked for a "gold, silver, and lavender" palette to convey Christmas joy. Took Joyce over three days to throw together a prototype to forward to Will and the clients for their consideration. This was *not* what she expected to hear during the meeting. Normally, Will would make a few suggestions. A touch up here. Swap out a stock photo there. Maybe clean up some edges that Joyce had planned on erasing anyway. This, though?

He was asking her to completely do it over again!

"You grew up with Christmas, right?"

Joyce was sure everything Will was about to say was in violation of *some* law, but she couldn't be assed to drag up the fact and let him keep talking. "Yes, Will," she said with a dour look. "I celebrated Christmas as a kid."

"So then you know the feeling they're going for."

"*What* feeling? What am I missing here?"

"That feeling of waking up Christmas day and rushing out of your bed to go open presents." Was that a prompt for her to light up and go, "*Oh, thank you, Will! I had totally forgotten!*" "Mom's in her PJs and Dad's pretending Santa took all the presents the night before! Stockings stuffed with candy and little cheap toys! Cinnamon rolls baking in the kitchen. The dog's losing its shit to go jump in the snow outside. Christmas carols bellowing out of the stereo. Grandpa in his awful sweater and grandma pinching your cheeks. *That's* the feeling the client wants to capture in their final marketing push of the season. Someone looking wistfully at their grandma because they didn't get the puppy they asked for isn't going to cut it. They want magic, wonder, and imagination."

Joyce pinched the bridge of her nose. Unfortunately for her, that was on full display for Will, who noticed her disdain from the moment she touched her own skin. "Some of us didn't have Christmases like that, Will."

"You know what I *mean,* though."

Joyce sighed again. While she didn't have many *bad* childhood Christmas memories, they were hard to think about now. *Stockings stuffed with toys?* Candy, sure, but what Joyce remembered best was scratch-off tickets that were about as fun as playing online poker for no gain. *Most I ever won was fifty bucks.* Joyce often thought that her mother could have used the twenty bucks in scratch-off tickets as actual presents, but hey, whatever made her mom happy. Same with the gaudy tinsel on the trees and *White Christmas* playing on loop on TV.

"One year I got up Christmas morning," Joyce began, elbow digging into the arm of her chair and fingers dancing upon her chapped lips, "and there was a big bicycle waiting for me by the front door."

"Uh huh. Good. Channel that en..."

"I walked right past it. Didn't care about getting a bike. Never asked for one, but my mom thought it was time for me to learn how to ride, I guess. I dunno. I must have been eight. Maybe nine. We lived out in the countryside. Where was I going to ride that bike? She never let me out of the driveway or our front yard. Learning to ride a bike on the grass? You have to be kidding me. We put training wheels on it and never took them off. I think I rode it three times, and one time was when a boy came over to visit and he made fun of me for my training wheels."

"Uh..."

"But yeah, Christmas. Like I said, I walked right by that thing. It was kinda ugly. Your standard 'girly' bike with purple and pink. This was the nineties, you know, so it was swamped with that washed out white and plastic tassels on the handlebars. I went straight to the TV, both of my parents saying, 'Is she blind?' They had put that bike out for me to find right away. They wanted a big show. They wanted me to be excited that I finally had a bike! Doesn't every kid want one? Then again, these were the same people who were shocked I didn't care about getting my driver's license when I turned sixteen. Was a total fluke I passed the fourth time I took my test, because I sure didn't care by that point." She had been twenty-four, and the only reason she put in any effort to get her license was so she could drive her mom back and forth to doctor's appointments when her aunt was too busy. "This is the kind of shit I think about when I remember Christmas morning. My parents being more disappointed than me."

"That's quite the story, Joyce." Well, she had him off his guard. Wasn't that Joyce's goal? Make this man who thought everyone had a universal Christmas experience realize the error of his foolish ways? "I, uh…"

"You know what?" She jerked up in her seat, chair squeaking and knee almost banging into the bottom of her desk. "Don't worry about it. I'll fix it. Christmas giving and wonder and joy. Only instead of green and red, it's gold, silver, and lavender. Got it. I'll make sure you have the new draft by the end of tomorrow."

"There was one other..."

"I've really gotta go to the bathroom, Will," Joyce lied, feigning her GI tract about to blow. "One nice thing about working from home all the time is that you don't have to deal with my IBS over Zoom."

"You have what now?'

Another lie, but he didn't have to know. Joyce killed the call and dropped her head against her desk, arms wrapping around her scalp and a sigh rattling the wood.

Why did she have to go and do something stupid like that? Will was one of her least favorite people to work with on a personal level, but he gave her consistent, good-paying work and usually went to bat for her above some of the other subcontractors. *It's hard to find people who will do that for you. Let alone people who don't actually like* you. Yet Joyce already knew why she lashed out like she had, with her rambling non-sequitur about a bike and her mother's incredulous disappointment.

Because fuck Christmas.

No, Joyce wasn't the type to bah-humbug her way through town. She had her favorite movies she liked to sit down and watch on good days. The scent of gingerbread and cinnamon brought a small smile to her face. Kids screaming about toys and Santa Claus waving to her in shopping malls wasn't the end of her world. Christmas? By itself? In her life?

She could live without it.

While she had no truly "bad" Christmases as a kid, the memories were now tainted. Her mother had been at the center of every one, fretting that she hadn't bought the right present or that her mother-in-law would make fun of her again that year. The one thing Joyce would never forget, though?

Her mother sitting in her bedroom, crying on Christmas Eve.

It had been the first Christmas following Joyce's grandmother's death. A death that had been a long time coming. Yet it didn't make that first Christmas any easier for the family, who had vowed to move on and make do with what they had. For Joyce's mother...

"I miss my Momma. I miss my Daddy."

Her mother had been in her late forties, yet she sat there and cried in the face of being an orphan at Christmastime.

What was that like?

I'm an orphan, too... Way younger than her mother had been. Hell, Joyce was way younger than her mother had been when she gave birth! Yet none of it meant anything to her. Was this what it was like to grieve differently from many people?

My father died one week before Christmas. My mother died one month before. What does it mean? She had been estranged from her father since her early childhood. Hadn't talked to him since she was in kindergarten. When she received the phone call, she felt absolutely nothing, which wasn't a surprise since she rarely thought of the man. The call about her mother, however?

She supposed it was because she had several years to prepare. The crying, the sobbing, and the bargaining with God had been done long ago. People called her resilient. That didn't make any sense to her. She was simply doing what was necessary to move on with life. There was nothing else to do.

Christmas, though...

Joyce hadn't celebrated in years. Not since her mother was diagnosed with dementia and had to be moved into the memory care facility where she lived out her lonely, boring days where she waged a war with her mind every morning and gave up by noon.

There was no point. Christmas was capitalism. It was a bastardization of whatever pagan holidays had been colonized hundreds, thousands of years ago. That's what Joyce told herself when she looked at parents shopping for Christmas presents and choked up a little.

None of it matters. It never mattered. Christmas isn't for single orphans, anyway.

Was it any wonder she agreed to go visit a woman on the coast? Getting out of Portland was imperative. The longer she hung around, the more Christmas decorations went up, and the more people on her neighborhood NextDoor conspired ways to celebrate together. Every day was an influx of emails about online stocking stuffer sales and where to order takeout to "keep local business alive." If that wasn't bad enough? Facebook, Reddit, and Twitter were full of local stories about people who had lost family members to the pandemic and would also be celebrating alone. Shouldn't those people feel shittier about Christmas than Joyce? Didn't feel right to sit in her cramped apartment and somehow convince herself she was anywhere near that scale of Grinchiness.

Going to stay with Abbie in Seaside was madness. Even outside of the pandemic, why would Joyce do such a thing? Hell, it would be their first time meeting in person, and doing it on such a pivotal holiday? Eh, made sense when she put it that way. *I have to get out of here. Not like anyone but me is at risk, anyway.* She came into contact with no one. If necessary, she wouldn't even go out for a walk for two weeks when she came back to Portland. Depending on how crazy it was on the coast. She heard all sorts of mixed messages about mask compliance outside of the metro area.

Yet Abbie still worked in a tourist shop. She still sat on restaurant patios and walked her dog on the beach when it swelled with people from the valley. Maybe going to visit her was a bad idea. Didn't Joyce have any concept of self-preservation?

I do... that's why I have to go. Staying cooped up in her apartment through Christmas, surrounded by cheer and misery while she chatted with people online sounded absolutely awful. Even if she tried to treat it as another day, it wouldn't work. There were reminders everywhere.

Reminders of pain. Of struggle. Of Christmases past that shouldn't matter anymore, but they did. Joyce couldn't even do her work without disappointing people. She didn't "understand" Christmas like normal people. Because she wasn't normal. She was an orphan without any family except that one estranged aunt she only talked to when it came to her mother's health.

Now she'd probably never hear from her aunt again. What was the point?

There is no point. There never was any point.

She'd go to Seaside, all right. She'd come out of her bubble and brave planting a kiss on another human's face. Not because it's what her mother would have wanted, per se, but because Joyce was desperate enough to get away from any and all reminders of a traditional family Christmas. It was the only way she was going to get any peace. Both in her heart, and in her soul.

Chapter 6

Two days before Christmas, Joyce packed into her car and loaded up Google maps on her phone. She already knew Abbie's address thanks to mailing her dirty photos and *other* things over the months, so that wasn't the problem. What ended up being the biggest annoyance was downloading enough podcast episodes to her phone to get her through the data dead zones winding along Highway 26, which connected Portland to Seaside. Or Cannon Beach, depending which direction a person turned once they reached Highway 101 on the coast.

Such a straight shot, wasn't it? Joyce was lucky that the woman she met lived in Seaside and not, say, *Coquille,* which would have been much longer – and tougher – to get to at that time of year. Luckily for Joyce, 26 hadn't been closed off yet due to weather. The rain was coming down pretty good, but she had changed the windshield wipers and had her tires checked. As long as she got out by one, she should get there before nightfall.

Should.

"Welcome to Reply All. A show about the internet." Joyce cranked up the volume on the stereo as she drove down the freeway that would eventually merge her onto Highway 26. Suburban Beaverton and Hillsboro flew by in a haze of drizzling rain and other dark cars splashing water against the pavement. Every time she passed someone, she had to turn up the stereo a little louder to hear people calling in about post-election results and what it meant to them. Billboards advertising insurance, Christmas savings, and the local megachurches reminded her why she was getting the hell out

of Portland for the next week or so. *I still have some work to do before Christmas, but by God, it won't be done in my office.* She also brought extra Vitamin D and enough hand sanitizer to bring Christmas joy to all of Seaside.

But did she remember what to do if she hydroplaned on a wet freeway?

"Jesus!" That *zzzrk!* sound as the tires were no longer hers to control gave her a minor heart attack. Yet life continued on a few seconds later, her eyes wide, face pale, and the podcast continuing to take calls. *My life flashed before my eyes...* No, it hadn't, but it sounded good, didn't it? Only if Joyce meant *endless Zoom calls and groceries delivered to my door* as her life flashing before her dried-out eyes.

She could hardly measure time as it slowly eked by. The more she left the metro area, the more she encountered the strange sights of the countryside. That one random Dairy Queen on the side of the road. The giant American flags flapping in the rain. Signs equally spaced out, telling everyone to "visit Sunset Coffee!" if they were on their way to the beach. The giant, random truck stop packed with cars. Joyce always wondered about that place. What was the deal? Was it mostly locals or tourists? Was this where all the country folk came to blow off steam and get a hot meal?

Soon, it was in the rearview mirror and out of Joyce's mind. She was also officially in the "dead" zone, now. Her phone knew to jump to the next downloaded podcast episode, and Google Maps worked well enough offline, but Joyce was such a product of modern city living that she always got that jolt of anxiety whenever she realized she didn't have any data. The giant R on her phone didn't instill confidence, after all. What if she was run off the road? What if she got lost? Would Google still work if she had to take a detour? Where even *was* she? The sky was getting darker for only 2:30. The last text she received from Abbie was to confirm she would be home from work that day and to come straight to the door.

What am I doing?

Now wasn't the time for turning around. A line of cars was behind Joyce. More were in front of her. Did everyone have the same idea about spending Christmas on the coast? Did this always happen, or did 2020 make people think, *"Eh, rather be on the empty, rainy beach than walking through my crowded neighborhood?"*

Fuck if Joyce knew. She was too busy trying to focus on the road and not feel guilty about doing something that felt so right in her soul.

Soon, she would be with Abbie. They would consummate everything they had built together over the past several months. The internet wouldn't be the only way they knew each other. Most of all... Joyce would not be alone that Christmas. Someone to touch. Someone to kiss. Physical reminders that there was love in the world, and she could partake, if careful.

Presents slid in the backseat whenever she took sharp turns. The rain did not let up. *Good thing I got those windshield wipers replaced.* They had been squeaking only two months ago. With the winter rains coming, Joyce couldn't stand the sound if they got worse. She wanted to focus on everything Abbie had promised her.

Hot food. A hot bed.

Was it possible to blush if someone were traveling by themselves? Of course it was. Why wouldn't it be!

"Ugh. You're a mess." Guilt on one shoulder and desire on the other. A COVID, Christmastime booty call. That's what this was.

When she finally broke through the rain and saw the signs pointing to either Seaside or Cannon Beach, she had a sudden flashback to her mother sitting in this exact spot, telling her daughter, *"Which way should we go? Doesn't matter in the end. We'll have fun either way."*

For some reason, Joyce couldn't remember which town they had traveled to all those years ago. Even when a girl was from the coast, the towns ran together when one had seen enough of them. Some were more touristy than others. More fishing oriented than others. Yet they were all essentially the same Oregonian town, for better or worse.

A horn honked behind her. It was Joyce's turn to merge, but she had been so lost in her memories that she wasn't paying attention.

She turned right, heading north to Seaside.

The signs were everywhere. For every one that made Joyce's heart flutter, there was another that filled her with dread. *What if it doesn't work out? What if we have no in-person chemistry? What if I'm really botching our Christmas?* This was when she had to pay the most attention to the map on her phone. She didn't know the layout of Seaside at all. It had been *years* since she last came through this way. Was this even the same town she remembered, or was she thinking of Cannon Beach? Newport? Freakin' Florence?

Calm down, you anxious, quarantine-breaking slut. She almost missed the turn toward the beach. Cars littered the highway and the side streets crossing the river that ran through the center of town. One of the streets was closed for "winter repairs" and Joyce had to find another way around. *I know what that means.* That street wouldn't be fixed until June.

She didn't see the beach before arriving at Abbie's one-story cottage, snug between a craftsman and a Queen Anne that had seen better days in this weather-worn town. Yet she certainly heard the ocean when she stepped out and felt a small splatter of rain against her face.

It sounded like construction work. That's how acclimated Joyce had become to city life after growing up in a tiny coastal town.

The smell of salt in the air.

The splashing mud puddles as trucks drove through them. *Trucks,* not sedans and SUVs.

Seagulls crying in the distance.

It was like a completely different world. In Portland, life revolved around craft beer and hiking – sometimes in that order. Here on the coast, though, everything drove people west toward the beach. Sunshine? Surf and sand. Rain and wind? Jackets and boots on the compact sand. Dogs had a great time either way. Kinda like the dog that soon ran up to the fence separating Joyce from Abbie's property, aptly named *Greywood Getaway* on a handmade plaque by the gate.

"Hey!"

That familiar head of dirty blond emerged from the glowing gold of the front doorway.

Joyce would recognize that baggy white sweater anyway, but she wasn't prepared for the light blue skinny jeans clinging to lean legs and slip-on shoes that squelched against the damp earth when Abbie leaped out of the doorway. She didn't bother to cover her head or her torso as she trotted down the short concrete path and met Joyce at the fence.

"You made it!"

Joyce, who instinctively put on her cloth mask before getting out of the car, recoiled from someone coming straight for her personal space. It took her more than a second to remember that she had come here on purpose, never mind to actually *touch* this person at some point. "Yeah. I did." Joyce bundled herself up in her coat and tucked her purse closer to her chest. "Good to see you. Guess this is really happening."

Abbie looked beyond Joyce's shoulder. Beside her, the dog yelped and jumped at the prospect of a guest in *their* space. *That dog is a lot bigger than I thought it would be.* Louder, too. Was it always this loud over video chat?

"Where are your bags? I'll carry them. Come on! I just got done Lysoling the place."

"Is that a word?" Joyce backed up against her chair, fumbling with the backdoor handle. "Or is it going to become one before the end of the year?"

"Come on! Before we get drenched!"

"Isn't this the perfect weather for the beach?" Joyce wasn't about to say no to concierge service. While Abbie reached into the backseat and gathered presents into her arms, Joyce followed her in the hopes that she wouldn't have to fend off the dog. Although they hurried toward the door, she took a moment to lock her car, still precariously parallel parked along the sidewalk. Here was hoping there weren't any yellow or red lines there that she couldn't see.

The dog beat them both inside. As soon as it stood in the small entryway, it shook off every last drop of rain in time for its owner to chastise its bad manners and for Joyce to debate asking if it were a boy or a girl. She vaguely recalled the name "Sammy," but that didn't help!

"Whew! You made it!" Abbie raised her arms high into the air after locking the front door. Joyce wasn't in a hurry to move. She was too busy taking in the sight of Abbie's sweater lifting up her abdomen... and the view of the little house in Seaside.

On a sunny summer day, it would have been perfectly picturesque. The bright yellow walls and light wood floorboards were a recent addition to a house that was probably at least fifty years old. The kitchen was decent for a house – still way bigger than Joyce's. The short hallway leading to the bathroom and two bedrooms were as Abbie had described them, and what Joyce had seen every time she was given a video tour of the place.

The biggest difference from what Joyce anticipated? *So many Christmas decorations!*

Garland lined the doorways. Lights twinkled in the dining area. A dancing Santa was placed on the dining table. Two stockings hung above the fireplace. The TV played a video of a yule log burning brightly. Some cinnamon-nutmeg candle burned somewhere, but Joyce couldn't find it. All she saw was the Christmas tree propped up in the corner of the living room, homemade and store-bought ornaments hanging alongside brightly-colored lights that flickered in ways Joyce couldn't comprehend.

"Welcome to Casa de Greywood!" Abbie's arms were still above her head. The presents had been left on the dining room table, soon to be added to the Christmas tree. "Wow... may I say that you are really gorgeous in *person?*"

Joyce rounded on Abbie. "Excuse me?"

"Oh... uh..." Sheepish Abbie would have charmed Joyce any other time. This was not a normal time, however. Joyce was either on the verge of passing out from the overwhelming sensations consuming her, or about to run back out to her car and grip the steering wheel to pull herself back together. "Sorry. Was that inappropriate? I've spent all of today wondering how I should address you when you got here. I mean, we flirt and do *all* sorts of stuff on the internet, but this is real life, you know?" When Joyce still wasn't responding, Abbie rubbed the side of her head and forced a grin. "Hi."

Finally, Joyce snapped out of her stupor. "Hi! I made it! I'm here!"

The anxiety visibly evaporated from Abbie's face. "Let me show you the guest room so you can get comfortable. Are you hungry?"

Joyce pulled her rolling suitcase behind her as she followed Abbie down the short hallway and to the left. "I guess. I ate right before I left, but it was oatmeal and yogurt. Sometimes it lasts most of the day, other times I'm famished long before dinner."

A welcoming smile brought Joyce into the cozy smaller bedroom, furnished with a full-sized bed and a dresser. The view was nothing more than the side of the craftsman's blue walls next door – and the rain continuing to pound against the glass – but it was already roomier and more refreshing than the apartment Joyce had been stuck in for most of the year. *Never thought I could hate my apartment so much until this year.*

"How about I make us some grilled cheese?" The dog appeared behind Abbie, tail wagging. When Joyce couldn't take her eyes off Sammy,

Abbie turned around and said, "You wanna meet Joyce, huh? Oh, now that you can smell her, she's suddenly real! Go figure!"

"Pardon me, but... well, I know this doesn't really matter in the realm of the world, but..." Joyce cleared her throat and tugged on the strap to her mask. "I can't remember your dog's gender."

"Huh? Oh! Sammy's a girl. A very friendly girl, although if you're not careful, she'll jump up on you and get her muddy little paws all over your nice sweater. Come on, girl! Let's go make those sandwiches!"

It took Joyce a short moment to realize that those words were directed at the dog, and not at her. That's how rattled she was already. *I keep thinking she's talking to me like I'm the dog.* Joyce sat on the edge of the bed and removed her mask. After inhaling a deep breath, she told herself that she was now committed to staying here with Abbie.

This would either be the longest week of her life, full of consequences she could both foresee and not...

Or this would be exactly what she needed most. Yet the more she thought about those Christmas decorations and the hyperactive dog ready to greet her at any moment, Joyce stopped thinking about the potential for human touch. All she saw in her head was the very thing she attempted to escape from in Portland.

Chapter 7

Abbie took a detour on the way to work the next morning. She stopped inside one of the shops on the same street as hers, saying hello to the woman behind the counter and an early Merry Christmas to the neighbor on her way out the door.

"Hey!" The owner, a woman named Rita, flagged down Abbie. "Wasn't expecting to see you here on today of all days! What's a wretch like you doing here on Christmas Eve?"

Abbie could only chuckle as she stayed a respective distance away from Rita, the only woman near the promenade who could talk to everyone like she already knew them and get away with it. "I need some last-minute Christmas decorations before tomorrow. I have a special guest staying with me for the holidays. I gotta get something that matches her aura, you know?" She knew Rita would know what she meant by that. This was a woman who would read your horoscope one moment and your tarot cards the next. *Not like everyone couldn't guess from the crystals hanging from her neck.* Abbie didn't mind. Part of the fun of living in a town like Seaside was knowing all of the eclectic shopkeepers who kept the town running both during and outside of tourist season.

"Christmas decorations? This late in the game?" Rita rounded the counter, and Abbie had to take another step back. *So many people around here can't mind their personal space even during the best of times.* "All right. Let me see what I've got. I'll even give you the post-Christmas clearance discount."

What Abbie didn't mention was how this was a Hail Mary pass after an awkward night with Joyce. While she knew things might be a little weird at first, she wasn't expecting her girlfriend to be so withdrawn and distant. After Joyce got settled into the guest room, she joined Abbie in the dining area to have their grilled cheese sandwiches. Sammy managed to behave the whole time they chatted and ate their late lunch. Yet the conversation didn't really go anywhere. Every time Abbie prompted Joyce to say something, she was met with a faraway look and the feeling that Joyce may have already regretted coming to visit. *I knew there probably wouldn't be any fooling around last night, but a girl still had hope.* To be fair, Abbie wasn't really feeling it either. Not after the bulk of their conversations revolved around giving away the Wi-Fi password and showing Joyce where everything was in the bathroom. *She smelled like spring blossoms...* That was Abbie's main take away after spending some time in Joyce's personal space. Something she couldn't get through a computer screen. What could she get, though? Memories of all the times they spent together on their Friday night dates doing God knew what.

Abbie had seen her girlfriend naked a hundred times, but it was so different standing in the same room together.

That morning, Abbie had reminded Joyce that she had to go to work one more time before Christmas. Joyce had set up her travel laptop in the living room, so she could watch TV and do some graphic design work. Abbie encouraged her to go for a walk at the beach before it got too dark, but Joyce made it sound like she would be working for most of the day. Something about having to completely redo a social media design graphic from the ground up.

What else could Abbie do but think of ways to add a little magic to their situation? She knew that Rita's shop would have something with the right kitschy theme to put a smile on Joyce's face. *Clearly, what I need is more Christmas. Everyone loves Christmas. God knows I need all the Christmas I can get this year!* Abbie was almost too tickled to realize that she wouldn't be alone that year. Her family may have only been a Zoom call away, but it was nowhere near the same as sharing a cup of cocoa and getting beneath a big, fuzzy blanket together. *I really hope we don't regret it...*

Too late for that now!

"How about this?" Rita slammed a motorized Santa on the counter. Before Abbie could ask what the hell was going on, Rita flipped a switch, and Santa was soon getting up on his feet, swaying back and forth, and mumbling the lyrics to "Holly Jolly Christmas."

"Er..." Abbie didn't know how to politely ask that this thing be taken out back and chucked into a dumpster. "Not sure she'll be into that. I mean, it's cute, Rita, I *love* it, but Joyce is the kind of person who is... um... a little more cosmopolitan."

"Riiiight." Rita shut off Santa and shoved him unceremoniously to the side. "You said she was from Portland. Woof."

Abbie hesitated. She knew exactly what she was getting into when she next spoke, but could hardly hold herself back. "What's that mean?"

"You know those big city types. Can't have any fun unless it involves quinoa and vegan leather. Get them coming into my shop every other day to ask me where they can get vegetarian food at a restaurant. I ask you, are French fries not vegetarian? These bozos can get whatever meatless food from McDonald's, as much as I care."

"I'm not actually sure if the McDonald's fries are..." Abbie bit back her words. "You know what? Maybe I'll play some music. Everyone loves Christmas music, right?"

Rita braced her hands against her glass counter, contemplatively chewing the side of her tongue. "That's one thing to say, I guess."

Right. Most people were sick of Christmas music. Surely, though, Joyce would appreciate a little extra cheer?

Abbie stepped out of the shop with a sigh. As she wandered into work, Sid was already clocked in, setting up some last minute signs detailing the sales and bargains found within. *I've already checked over everything in here.* Nothing screamed, "Take me home to your new girlfriend!" Too bad. Abbie was starting to get desperate.

"Hey, hey!" Sid, sitting atop a ladder to hang up the post-Christmas clearance signs, waved to her from his perch. "How's it going, lady killer? Your girl show up yesterday? Or did she back out at the last minute?"

Abbie placed her bag in a drawer behind the counter and removed her scarf, hat, and gloves. The heat was up plenty inside the shop, but it took more than a few minutes for her cold body to acclimate to work temperatures. *Did I turn on the heater at home before I left?* What if Joyce woke up to a frigid house or, worse, a *cold toilet?* That toilet could get pretty cold if Abbie didn't turn on the heater by the hallway and keep the bathroom door open for a few hours.

"She's there. Left her sleeping in the guest room."

"Oh..." Sid's shoulders drooped. "Guest room, huh?"

"What, you think we're banging the first night she comes to visit?"

"I mean... you were pretty excited about that possibility."

Abbie slammed her elbows on the counter and tapped her fingers against her cheeks. "I knew things would be a little weird. We've spent the past few months only talking online. Normally, we would have met long before this, right? In the BC times, that is."

"If that means 'before corona,' then I catch your drift." Sid put the finishing touches on the sign and helped himself down the ladder. He checked for drafts around the front door before folding up the ladder and pushing it to the side. It was still too early to flip the OPEN sign, and Sid liked to take his time cleaning up every day. "So, things are weird?"

Abbie sighed. "I get the feeling she's not telling me something. All evening she was pretty cagey. Kept asking me questions about myself and the house, but it wasn't like... *genuine*. Thought she might want to go for a walk on the beach, but she looked at me like I was crazy for suggesting it. Girl's from Oregon. I know she's mentioned growing up down the coast."

"Whoa, really? Whereabouts?"

"I dunno. Bandon? Coos Bay?"

"Damn. Bandon's good beaches. Coos Bay...?" Sid shrugged, slamming some of his tools onto the counter. "Not so much."

"You're a connoisseur of Oregon beaches?"

"Why do you think I settled in Seaside? I had my pick of towns looking for handy types."

"Yet you settled in *Seaside,* and have a job at a shop."

"Hey... I mean..." Another sheepish shrug. "Times are tough. When I moved here several years ago, I really did have my pick!"

"Seaside is known for its convenient beaches, which is why my parents always came here." It was true, unfortunately. If someone wanted to hit up a beach on the fly, Seaside was a convenient town to visit. Bam. Beach right there! Literally feet away from most hotel doors! Yet that high-traffic over the decades meant the beach was flat and picked clean. Oh, and packed. Lest Abbie forget why she usually took Sammy for beach walks late in the winter evenings or early summer mornings, when the place was its most cleared out.

"We're getting off topic here," Sid said. "Tell me, is Joyce as pretty in real life as she is in the pictures you've shown me?"

Abbie couldn't hold back her laugh. "Yes. She's gorgeous. Rolled up into my house wearing jeans and a baggy jacket, and all I could think about was how beautiful she was." Another sigh. "Look, I knew nothing was going to happen last night." She had never told Sid about the *naughty* stuff that happened on those Friday night dates, but he had probably picked up on the tone of her voice and the giddiness in her throat every time she went home for the week. *We were totally cyber-banging.* Totally. "But I expected *something.* Stroll on the beach. Walk around the neighborhood. Cuddling on the couch watching TV..."

"Abbie, you gotta think about one difference between you and her, based on everything you've told me. You've spilled *plenty* of beans."

Incredulous, Abbie crossed her arms and allowed him to continue.

"She's been stuck inside, without real life human interaction, for a long-ass time. Since, like, March. Meanwhile, you may not be seeing as many people, but life has kinda gone on as usual for you here."

"I don't recall hugging you lately."

"Nooo, but you still see and talk to me in the flesh. That's a lot more than your Joyce can say." He gathered up his tools before they scratched the glass counter. "She might be a bit shell-shocked after this crazy year. I mean, she's from Portland! They've had all manner of bullshit. Between the protests and the virus... oh, and all the damn smoke. Girl may have stayed inside the whole time, but that kinda makes it worse, right? Nobody to hug you, nobody to kiss you... hell, nobody to high-five you! Most people can't live like that for very long before it starts messing with their heads."

He turned around, tools in his hands. "I've gotta go dither around in the back. Holler if you need anything."

"Maybe a reset button on yesterday!" Abbie called after him. "Losing my mind a bit!"

Either he didn't respond, or she didn't hear him. Regardless, Abbie had five minutes to herself before flipping the sign and pretending she was already hard at work on Christmas Eve.

She pulled her cell phone out of her pocket and checked for a message from Joyce. Nothing. She was probably still in bed.

"*Good morning, gorgeous. Hope you're feeling a little better today and more rested. I'll bring us home some takeout for dinner when I get off at five. We're closing early tonight, but not early enough for a walk on the beach. You should go! I left a spare key on the table by the door. You can hang onto it as long as you're here. Love...*" Abbie erased that last word. She may have texted that before yesterday, but now was not the time. "*Take care. Let me know if you need anything. I work only ten minutes away.*"

As soon as she hit send, she turned the OPEN sign around and spotted a regular standing outside the door. Abbie adjusted her mask straps and unlocked the latch with a hidden smile on her face. Work had begun.

Chapter 8

Although she knew she was alone in the house, Joyce took her time rolling out of bed. Her foot smacked into one of her overnight bags she had left lying next to the nightstand. As soon as she shook off the pain, she took her phone to the bathroom across the hall and immediately noticed the big, uncovered window looking into the neighbor's yard.

Right. People have windows in their bathrooms. She hadn't possessed one of those ever in her life. Not even her childhood home had a window in the bathroom. Every apartment in the city? Nope. When a woman never had to worry about peeping toms, she got comfortable waltzing into bathrooms and sitting down on the toilet without thinking.

Not today. She had enough wherewithal to unhook the curtain and cover up the window, although the odds of someone staring through the window while she peed were probably slim to none. If nothing else, she hid her shame when she plopped down onto the porcelain and was instantly met with the biting cold sensation of an icy toilet against her ass cheeks.

Her phone fumbled from her hands and landed with a soft "plop" on the bathroom rug in front of the shower. Grumbling, Joyce plucked it up and noticed a text from Abbie. Something about there being a key, and that she wouldn't be back until dark. With takeout.

Joyce hadn't thought about what she wanted to do with her day. Not yet. She was taking things one hour at a time.

Mostly because she knew that as soon as she looked out at the clear day, a rush of feelings would overwhelm her.

She kept her back to the front windows while eating a breakfast of oatmeal and yogurt she had brought with her from Portland. Her eyes were only for her phone, which was littered with tawdry Reddit posts, glaring Christmas photographs on Instagram, and so many tweets about *Stay the Fuck Home* that Joyce had to shut the thing down before she got a headache.

After putting her one dirty dish in the sink, she propped her laptop up on the coffee table in the well-lit living room and debated turning on the TV. Too bad she couldn't figure out how the remote worked, leaving her to drink a can of soda from the fridge while scrolling through Facebook and finally checking her emails. A few Christmas wishes, and Joyce had to admit it was time to start working.

If only her Dropbox would fucking sync.

As much as she hated to admit it, she was stuck looking out the window while her laptop sorted itself out. Joyce couldn't work on the social media marketing project until the files synced and she had her templates back in her possession.

Oh... guess you can't see the ocean from here. Only the neighbor's house across the street, and a six-story hotel a couple blocks behind it. Seagulls swept in and out of view, but the only other reason Joyce even knew she was so close to the beach was because every other yard on the block had some repurposed rowboat and a myriad of references to "Life's Better on the Beach."

She always thought that phrase was highly debatable.

Work distracted her well into the afternoon. Yet every time Joyce thought she had finally made strides with a company's post-Christmas projects, she was reminded that, yes, it was Christmastime. Didn't help that every time she looked up from her laptop, she was met with garlands, lights, and a tree that waved to her from the corner of the room. The presents she had brought were added beneath it. Some of them were labeled for her. While that put a tiny smile on Joyce's face, she forced herself to focus on her work so most of it would be finished before Abbie came home with dinner.

As things naturally go, though, Joyce became restless. While there was plenty more room in this small house than her Portland apartment, Joyce concluded that since she was in a new town on a nice-ish day, she was doing herself a disservice by not going out for a socially-distanced walk and seeing what the big hubbub was about Seaside. After all, every other Portlander insisted that it and Cannon Beach were *the* places to go!

Joyce closed her laptop lid and pulled a heavy sweater over her turtleneck. Her walking shoes also happened to be her driving shoes, and were left by the front door. With a heavy cloth mask on her face and gloves on her hands, Joyce picked up the key left for her on the small table by the front door and ventured into the increasingly cloudy day.

She was instantly hit with the smell of the beach.

Eyes closed and hair gently whipping into her face, Joyce made sure the door was locked behind her before venturing out into the street. Thunder crashed in the distance. *No, that's the ocean.* Salt lingered in her nose. The squawking seagulls were louder out here. So were the kicking truck motors and tourist cars making the rounds toward the beach. Yet it was the ocean that drew Joyce's curiosity the most. That familiar, long-ago sound that she associated with the bulk of her childhood living on the coast. *It's been so long since I've been to the beach.* Each step brought her closer to turning the corner on the block. Joyce vaguely remembered what direction the house faced, but she would know which way to go, regardless. The taller buildings on the horizon and the gulls in the air advertised the sea.

The closer she got to turning that corner, the closer to her body she held her sweater, as if bracing herself for the wave of emotions she'd feel.

She turned. The vague, gray outline of the sea was in the distance.

Did it call to her? Not really. There was no, *"Joyce... Joyce... this is your destiny..."* If anything, Joyce was ignored. Maybe cajoled by the seagulls, who saw her for the native daughter she was. *"Here's this bitch again,"* they seemed to say, *"late, as usual. Can you believe how many years it has been? Her mother was still fairly cognizant the last time they came here!"*

Joyce ignored the screaming seagulls and the cars roaring down the street. Her focus was on the beach, and hopefully not the people milling back and forth as they took turns walking by in their masks and hats firmly on their heads. Joyce was so focused on the road beneath her feet and the crashing waves on the horizon that it was either that or obsess over the memories slowly claiming her sanity.

The last time I went to the beach... Her mother had been with her. One of the rare times she checked her mother out of the memory care facility and took her for a ride in the car. *I drove her through McDonald's and bought her a Big Mac and Fries, because that's what she always wanted.* Diet Coke for days. A Hershey bar as dessert. In the end, Joyce's mother had become so addicted to sugar that everyone in her life decided to let her have at it. *"I'll be honest with you, Ms. Stewart,"* the head nurse at the facility had candidly said, *"it's one of the only things that makes her happy. In my experience, those at the end of their life might as well have whatever vices makes them happy for one more day. If she wants to eat nothing but Twinkies and drink nothing but Diet Coke, let her.*" So they did. Fast food whenever they left the facility. A healthy budget for staff to buy Joyce's mother whatever candy she wanted.

Joyce supposed she didn't have to pay for that any longer. Her mother was gone, and so was her bottomless appetite for all things chocolate, sweet, and sugary.

I still remember the way she vapidly stared at the ocean.... Every time Joyce tried to have a conversation, her mother responded with, "*I want to go home.*" Or, even better, "*Where's my mom?*" A woman who had been dead for twenty years by that point. Joyce had barely been in kindergarten when her grandmother died, but in that car, she was the only one who knew that.

"*Grandma's visiting my aunt in Minnesota.*" That was the story everyone regurgitated, because aside from giving her whatever food she would eat? The last thing Joyce wanted to do was tell her mother that someone had been dead for twenty years. There was no point. Only pain.

Joyce stopped one block away from the beach. She reminded herself that this one was far different from the one near her mother's memory care facility. Different view. Different people. Totally different vibe, thanks to all of the touristy crap right up on the promenade.

Hell, the fact there was a promenade!

"Wow." Joyce had reached the edge of town, where concrete turned to sand. To her left and right was an endless stretch of sidewalk. Before her? The vast, flat ocean that churned upon itself every time it remembered to follow its own tides. The beach was so flat, so sparse that it hardly looked like the beaches Joyce grew up by down south. The few people traipsing across the sand were bogged down in winter clothes and carrying dog toys. Flags fluttered in the harsh winter breeze. Behind her, the branded hotels offered balcony views and personal lounging space for those who didn't want to get caught up in the rabble.

Are those... swing sets?

Joyce counted one, then two, both of them empty upon the beach. Farther down was a foot washing station, as well as maps and memorials for the area. Everything about Seaside was far fancier than anything Joyce experienced in southern Oregon, where one was lucky to have a traversable path down the steep hills to the untamed beaches. *From the looks of it, there isn't a single shell or agate to pick up down there.* The sand was so compact that she wouldn't have to worry about her feet sinking into hidden dunes or her shoes filling up with hot, dusty sand.

Was this even the same state she grew up in?

Either things have changed, or I can't remember things correctly. Joyce took a few tentative steps out onto the sand. Although she wore her crappiest shoes, she still worried that they might get a little too dirty before she left. That's what it was like growing up back home. Joyce had never been a fan of the beach. As a child, she never learned how to swim due to a near drowning incident in a hotel swimming pool. Although her hydrophobia wasn't as bad now as it used to be, she still had never learned how to swim. Looking out at the tumultuous waves, she thought about how easy it would be to get caught up in a riptide. *Not that I'm saying I want to. Sounds like an awful way to die.* There were many awful ways to die, including slowly losing one's memories and forgetting who they used to be before the disease finally came for them.

The few times she went to the beach as a kid, Joyce got hung up on the annoying sand trapped in her sandals, the rocky shorelines she had to traverse with her family, the dead sea mammals that had washed up with the tide, and avoiding touching anything that might be the slightest bit gross. Her parents often scolded her for caring so much about what they believed to be such trivial matters. Yet how many times had she forced herself to go on those little adventures, hoping to convince herself that she really liked it this time?

Looking up and down the beach here in Seaside, Joyce realized it truly wasn't anything like she was used to growing up. No rocks. No dead animals. No small pools full of sea creatures, ready to gross her out if she got too close. Just a swing set, and the endless foam washing up upon the shore.

Everything about this beach was stark, empty, and sanitary. The tourists who came here didn't see the Oregon Joyce knew. They saw the carefully curated world made for them, the playground for those who lived on the other side of the Coast Range.

Joyce couldn't say she hated it, though. The less it reminded her of troubled memories, the more likely she was to walk down the beach without a care in the world. She didn't even care that a mixture of sea spray and rain tickled her face. If anything, it felt natural. Cleansing.

When Abbie comes back tonight, we should talk about what we want from my visit. There. Much more pleasant to think about. After all, Joyce had come here not only to get away from the city, but to spend some quality time with the girlfriend she met on the Internet. A woman she had no problem doing all sorts of things with when they happened online. *Maybe that's my problem. Everything felt safer when it only happened between screens.* Joyce could hide away her emotions. Pretend nothing bothered her. When Abbie had direct access to her in the flesh, things changed. Joyce had already noticed her barriers erecting and her mood souring at the idea of being at the mercy of another woman's intuition. Abbie was as sweet and pretty in real-life, but it came with a price. If Joyce wanted to hold her, kiss her, and maybe share a bed with her, she had to expose her heart to the woman she was falling in love with. Unfortunately, that heart was filled with a kind of grief that remained frozen in time.

For a few minutes, though, Joyce emptied her mind and allowed herself to become one with the environment. Nobody here knew her. They didn't know her past, or what a place as simple as the beach meant to her. Perhaps there were other people here who likewise had complicated histories that nobody else could conceive, but Joyce didn't have to worry about them, and they didn't have to worry about her. They minded their own business. They left her to her own.

When she came back to the place where her walk began, she hesitated before ascending the steps to the promenade. One of the empty swing sets caught the attention of her eye. How long had it been since she last enjoyed fun on the swings? They had once been her favorite playground game, but elementary school had been a long, long time ago.

Joyce grasped the metal chain dangling from the frame. *Seems sturdy to me...* Slowly, she stood in front of the swing, arms wrapping around the chains as she sat down and allowed gravity to do the rest. While not the most comfortable seat, Joyce had a wonderful view of the ocean. The endless expanse would soon welcome the sun, drowning it in gray waves that were as bare as the scenery. *Ah, I see. That's what looks wrong. There are no fishing vessels out there.* Further proving that everything about this stretch of shoreline was sanitized.

Joyce didn't care. As she kicked her feet back and forth, the swing gaining a little air, she imagined what it would be like to gain so much momentum that she was flung into the sea and dissipated into careless foam and spray. Perhaps, somewhere out there, was her mother's soul dancing in the water and hoping to see her one last time.

The thrill of being on a swing set for the first time in decades overshadowed the other feelings swelling within her heart. This way, Joyce didn't have to acknowledge the tears shedding from her eyes. The wind and rain took care of them for her.

Chapter 9

Abbie came home to an empty house. The key by the front door was gone, and so was Joyce. Although Abbie had managed to get off work twenty minutes early, it was still dark by the time she reached home. She had assumed Joyce would be there. Her car was there, so she had not driven anywhere. Abbie hoped she was having a safe walk around town.

Meanwhile, she would plate the take-out she brought with her. Salads and French fries soon decorated the dining table. Naturally, that wasn't all. Abbie had another trick up her sleeve to set the mood with her girlfriend.

The door opened ten minutes later. There was Joyce, removing her gloves, scarf, and sweater. She looked up to see Abbie in the dining room and offered a friendly smile. It took Abbie a few seconds to get over how enchanting those rosy cheeks and fluffy hair looked.

"You're home!" Joyce locked the door behind her and said hello to Sammy as she ran up in greeting. "Sorry I was out so late. I went for a walk on the beach and then up and down the promenade. Looks like the perfect place for an early morning jog. Ever try it?"

Abbie shook her head. "You know I've told you I'm not one for running unless I'm late, but I see people out there all the time jogging back and forth like they have nowhere to go."

"That's because it's all about clearing their minds and revitalizing their bodies," Joyce said with a chuckle. "What do you have there?"

"Told you I was bringing home dinner. I thought salads were safe enough. Anything you don't want, you can take out and throw in mine. Also have a nice array of salad dressings in the fridge. I get a little something of everything every time I go out or order in, so I have quite the collection. You seem like an Italian dressing sort of woman. Or, maybe, honey Dijon ranch?"

Much to Abbie's relief, Joyce was still laughing. While Sammy danced around her, she approached the dining table and put her hands on the back of the chair, pushing out her chest and batting her eyelashes. "Believe it or not, I love salads, but don't care much for dressing. I eat all my salads dry."

"Are you kidding? Pretty sure that constitutes as sociopathic behavior." Abbie lured her dog to come join her at the end of the table. That gave Joyce some room to sit down in peace. "Whatever you want, though, my darling." She went back into the kitchen to get her own dressing. Abbie would be damned if she ate dry salad.

Joyce had an expectant look on her face when Abbie returned. As soon as they were both in their chairs, Joyce said, "Your darling, huh?" A fork tapped against her bowl. "I was wondering when you would get flirty."

"Are you saying I wasn't being flirty enough last night? Because I felt like I spent every moment between you getting here and going to bed trying to suggest that we get into each other's pants." Abbie held up the container of French fries. "Fried starch?"

Joyce did not readily take any. "Sorry about last night. I was really tired from the drive. I know it's not a very long one, but at this time of year, it can be quite harrowing. Had to take it easy while also maintaining constant vigilance of the road."

"Hey, you don't have to explain it to me. It's also your first time getting out of the city in a long while. Even before the pandemic, right?"

Joyce nodded. "Last time I got out of town had to be early last year. I drove down to Medford for a regional graphic design conference. I knew one of the organizers. He wanted me to do a talk about color theory. Little did I know, everyone who attended were either freshman college students, or little old ladies trying to pick up a side hustle." Joyce was soon lost in thought. "Come to think of it, it was the old ladies who had the best grasp of color theory. For a lot of them, it was the first time hearing about it. Go figure, huh?"

"That's my girl," Abbie said. "So badass she gives talks at conferences." She stabbed her fork into her salad, ranch dressing squishing against the side of her bowl, "I hope you're feeling a little bit better today after having a walk on the beach. Sorry I couldn't go with you, but you could have taken Sammy. She loves to go to the beach and can take care of herself around here. I hope she wasn't too much hassle today."

"I actually didn't see her. Honestly, I forgot you had a dog until I was already outside. She must have been asleep somewhere."

"If you didn't see her, that's because my neighbor stops by to give her walks throughout the day when I can't. You must have missed each other. Come to think of it, I didn't tell her that I would be having company this Christmas. Huh. Maybe I should have done that, what with his pandemic and everything."

Joyce looked down at her salad. "I saw lots of cute shops, but didn't go inside any of them. I don't know, guess I feel guilty about it. I already feel guilty enough about coming to visit during these times. You know..." Joyce slid her hand across the dining table, inviting Abbie to touch her. "I really missed that human connection you can only get in real life."

Abbie stared at her girlfriend's hand, wondering if her eyes were deceiving her. *Is this it? Are we going to hold hands like a real couple?* Slowly, Abbie placed her own hand on the dining table and pushed it forward until her fingertips touched Joyce's. While an impulse of adrenaline surged, Joyce offered her a warm, inviting smile. Soon, their fingers were fully entwined. Abbie could have stayed like that forever, except that was her dominant hand she needed to eat her dinner. Joyce, who was likewise right-handed, continued to munch on her salad and French fries. The only reason Abbie didn't reclaim her hand to eat, was because she was so smitten with that calm look that brought a renewed peace to the house.

"For what it's worth, I'm really glad you came." Abbie uncurled her fingers from Joyce's and picked up her fork again. "I've been wanting to see you for so long. Having you here for Christmas means so much to me. Like I told you online, I had made the hard decision to not visit my parents back home in Eugene this year. Sometimes, they come here to spend the holidays on the coast, but that obviously wasn't happening this year either. A part of me is really jealous that they still get to be together. I know they want me there, and maybe I would still go if circumstances were different... Except you know how my mom is. We can't risk it. It's one thing for me to take a chance, but I could never do that to my mom. Oh, that reminds me. Have you heard anything about your mother recently?"

Abbie knew enough about Joyce's mother to understand that it might be a delicate question. Yet it had been a while since Joyce did anything about it. *Last thing I remember was her getting a call that her mother had fallen down at the nursing home and had to go to the hospital.* The way Joyce talked about it, though, she was completely detached from it. As if her mother's well-being no longer existed in her consciousness. While Abbie would never fault her for the way she responded to things, it was completely foreign to someone who had never seen one of her parents go down that path. *My mother being sick was scary enough, but she was still my mother throughout the whole thing.* Listening to Joyce talk about the day she realized she would never have her mother again had pierced Abbie right in the heart. That was about two months into their relationship. *The day I realized she had been through some heavy shit that I cannot yet comprehend.* Sometimes, Joyce seemed so much older than Abbie. She had grown up much quicker out of necessity. Although, Abbie supposed that was also the difference between being an only child and the youngest of three. A part of Abbie felt like she never had to grow up. Joyce never had the choice. She had been alone and on her own since her early twenties.

Joyce was not quick to reply. She stirred some of her lettuce and picked up a piece of carrot that she nibbled on without thought.

"No, haven't heard anything recently. I always assumed that no news is decent news."

Abbie let out a sigh of relief. At least that was one less thing to worry about that Christmas. "I won't talk about it too much with you if it will bring down your mood. We can talk about anything we want. Can tell you everything about this town, my dog, or myself. I'm an open book."

Two hazel eyes narrowed in sultry seduction. One moment, Joyce was caught up in whatever thoughts had consumed her. Now? She was grabbing Abbie by the hand and biting her lower lip, like they would be going straight to dessert after this.

"I can ask you *anything*?" Joyce fluttered her eyelashes.

Abbie gulped. "Yup," she squeaked. "Sure can. Open book! Read me like the Bible."

"The Bible, huh? Open you up to the Song of Solomon and read to the congregation."

"Whoa, forgot about that one. Actually, I never went to church as a kid, so I don't get a lot of references."

"Neither did I." Joyce snorted. "I guess I only really have one question I wanna ask."

"What's that?"

Joyce hesitated. Was she drawing this out for the purpose of killing Abbie? Because it was working. "Don't suppose I can get some of your body heat tonight when we go to bed? Preferably together?"

A piece of lettuce fell from Abbie's mouth. Absolutely her smoothest move! "I, uh..."

"Don't worry, I've thought you plenty chivalrous since I got here." Joyce sipped from her glass of water. The way her lips pursed over the rim of her glass... *oof.* Abbie was already fantasizing about what it would be like to kiss those lips and *maybe* lead to something more. *It's not enough that I know what she looks and sounds like when she's in the throes of passion.* Abbie yearned to taste those lips and feel the sweet undulations of a body at the height of pleasure. Mostly the kissing – and the touching. From the day Joyce first took off her top on camera, Abbie had been wondering what it would be like to shove her face in that cleavage and wrap her tongue around either of those enticing nipples.

Somewhere beneath that turtleneck. Because of course Joyce was wearing a turtleneck.

"I'm sure that can be arranged." There it was! Abbie regathering her bearings and remembering how to flirt back. *Bit different with her beautiful face so close to mine. In real life.* Granted, Joyce was sitting several feet away, but that was much closer than she had been since they met! "Would be nice to have someone besides the dog in bed with me."

Joyce coyly pulled her bowl closer to her body as she rounded her shoulders and tucked her long, luxurious hair behind her ear. "When's the last time you had proper companionship in your bed, Ms. Greywood?"

Abbie cleared her throat, attempting to play it cool. Unfortunately, she cleared that throat so hard that she started to cough. As soon as she had some water down her throat, she said, "I've honestly never had anyone here before. I mean, I've dated a couple girls here and there, mostly tourists in town for the weekend... but it rarely went anywhere. Craziest it got was making out on the beach, but those tourist girls especially never want to commit to anything more. Feels great being that coastal fling."

"Well..." Joyce scooted a little closer, fingers soon ascending the length of Abbie's arm. "I'm not looking for a fling. I don't have time or emotional reserves for *flings*. I want someone more stable. Someone who can last me a good while, even if we're doing it long distance." Her whole body now pushed toward Abbie, whose eyes desperately wanted to see through that thick, black turtleneck taunting her from the other chair. "I don't lead women on. When I say I want to get into bed with them, I damn well mean it." A grin crossed her face. "I've got a bit of decent experience, too. Nothing you can do that will scare me off." Her lips were soon close enough to touch Abbie's ear, never mind whisper into it. "I even brought that little egg with me. You know, the one you control?"

Joyce pulled back and laughed as Abbie became so flustered that she hooted in embarrassment. *Only because of what she's doing to me!* Was there a part of Abbie's body that wasn't ready to jump those bones and go to town on the dining room floor? *It's been so long. So much waiting. Oh, my God. Can I truly wait any longer?*

She would have to, because Joyce returned to her seat and continued eating dinner like she hadn't said anything.

Abbie was the one who leaped up and did the few dishes they had when dinner was finished. Joyce followed her into the kitchen, head cocked to one side while Abbie furiously scrubbed the forks they had used to eat their dinners.

She's gonna come over here. Oh, my God. It's happening. Here she comes! Abbie was still scrubbing, pretending this was any ordinary Thursday night outside of Christmas eve, and nearly leaped out of her skin when Joyce stood right behind her and encircled both arms around her girlfriend's waist.

Abbie froze where she stood, hot water running over her hands while hot breath blew against the back of her neck.

"Wow. I've been wanting to do this for a *long* time." Joyce squeezed a little harder, enticing Abbie to finally turn off the sink and lean back into her girlfriend's hug. "You would come online wearing those baggy sweaters and all I could think was how cuddly you looked."

Abbie wetted her lips in anticipation. "Hopefully not *just* cuddly."

"Of course, you would often show up in lingerie, too, and all I could think was how much I wanted to shove you down onto your bed and do all *sorts* of unthinkable things to your body."

Both forks clattered into the sink. Was Abbie surprised when Joyce pulled her arms away and giggled behind her? No! Because this was exactly what she anticipated her girlfriend to be like in real life! *No matter how much she flirts, she's going to make me work for it.* Not like online, where Joyce was likely the first one out of her clothes and her fingers in places the sun couldn't reach. That's how some women were, though!

Merry Fucking Christmas to me!

"I'll be in the other room when you're done." Joyce folded her arms over her chest and pretended to pout on her way out of the kitchen. "Thanks for bringing dinner. It was delicious."

"You, uh, gonna turn on the TV?"

"Hm, no. I think I'll check my email one last time before waiting for you on the couch."

Waiting for me! On the couch! Well! Abbie wasn't about to say something that might ruin that. She would simply hurry up and get those forks in the dishwasher and her hands dried off before popping into the bathroom for some...

Ah, she had to get ready. Like making sure her hair looked presentable and her clothes weren't totally askew. When she went back out there, she was determined to be as sexy and put-together as whenever she sat down for a Friday-night date. It was the least she could do for the woman who had taken chances to come visit for Christmas. *She didn't have to come. We could have had a Zoom Christmas date.* Maybe there might be more Zoom in their future, but there didn't have to be that week.

Joyce had promised to stay a whole week. At least. This was Abbie's chance to make the most of it.

She stepped back out into the living room. Joyce sat on the couch, laptop in her lap while Sammy settled down for a nap by the fireplace. *I should light a fire.* No, it was plenty warm thanks to the heaters. *So I'll turn down the heaters.* Abbie attempted to sneak to the thermostat, but was caught by Joyce, who peered over the back of the couch and commented on what she had done with her hair.

"Did you do that for me?" Joyce sank farther into the couch. Soon, her laptop was closed and on the coffee table. "I like it. Keeps it outta your face for kissy times."

Abbie tapped her fingers together. "I did it in like thirty seconds."

"I like it, though. Why don't you come over here and taste your dessert?"

Abbie tested the bun on her head, making sure it wouldn't come crumbling down the moment things got a little *tumultuous* on the couch. One last time, she adjusted her sweater, hoping the collar wasn't engulfing her chin or the hem was stuck in her jeans. Only then did she approach the couch. Luckily for her, Sammy didn't get too excited – after dinner and a vigorous walk, the dog was ready to conk out for the evening.

"You're awfully flirty tonight." Abbie sat on the far end of the couch. "Guess you had a really good walk earlier. Was a good day for it, huh?"

Joyce scooted closer. "I don't mind a little rain in my face. Can even stand the wind if it's not too cold. Remember, I grew up on the coast. Suppose the only thing to throw me off was how everything looked." The seduction fizzled from her eyes, but only for a moment. "I'm not used to super smooth and flat beaches full of people. Or being able to walk *along* the beach. Where I'm from, it's all rocky outcrops and cliffs dunking you into the ocean if you're not driving carefully. Absolutely beautiful, but you have to work to get there."

"Yeah, well, I told you Seaside appealed to the valley people." Abbie shrugged. "It's good walking for those who don't have the best mobility. Lots of older people move here because they walk a long ways without being in too much pain."

Joyce pulled herself even closer. Soon, Abbie smelled that intoxicating perfume again. "As hot as this conversation makes me..." Her hand raised so suddenly that Abbie pulled back against the couch. "Why don't we cut to the chase?"

"Yeah, that walk really did you in. Made you horny, I see."

Joyce laughed, shoulder slumping against the back of the couch. "Are you saying you haven't been thinking about it since I got here?"

"Yeah..." Abbie didn't want to look too desperate, though. Joyce was the one putting herself out. And as Abbie had told her, she was used to women being into a few small things but bailing out on the bigger fun. Why would she take the chance of embarrassing herself any further than she already had? "Obviously I didn't want to pressure you to do anything. Just because you like doing some crazy shit over video chat, doesn't mean you're showing up and begging me to sleep with you."

"You can say the F word." To Abbie's mild surprise, Joyce sat up and pulled her turtleneck over her head. The fabric landed on the floor. Beneath it had been one of the bras Abbie had commented on the most over those past few months. *After I said I really liked it one time, I noticed she started wearing it more often for our dates.* The most frustrating thing was getting online and seeing Joyce in nothing but her sexy underwear. The longer their hot conversations went on, the more likely one of the straps were to loosen and fall down her arm. If she didn't pull it back up, at some point her nipple would poke out of its cup. That was the stuff!

Here it was! Right in front of Abbie!

"Fuck?"

Joyce's eyes slightly widened, but she soon fell into another fit of laughter. "When are you going to kiss me?"

"I didn't know it had to be so one-sided! Man, this is so much pressure. I feel like a teen boy in the closet for a game of Seven Minutes in Heaven."

"We could go in the closet if you want. Oh, oh. What would you have done with me if we were teens playing that game? Come on. I wanna hear."

"Really?" Wow, this really was like one of their online dates. *Talking about nothing. Then talking about sexy things. Then taking off our clothes and getting off in front of our cameras.* If Abbie were lucky, there would be another half hour afterward of them lying on their beds and gazing into their webcams. "Guess we'd have to kiss, yeah?"

"Two teenagers kissing. Could go either way."

"Definitely feel you up. I'd probably have been spending half the night trying to not get caught staring at your chest. I'd take it as my opportunity to go for second base."

Joyce's face was now so close that Abbie could have easily kissed her. "What's stopping you? You can do whatever you want to me." There went the strap! And the other one! Whoa, on purpose? *Good thing I closed the curtains at dark!* The neighbors didn't need to see this. *I mean, they totally do, but only because they need to see how unbelievably lucky I am.* "Whatever you've been fantasizing about every time you watched me come on camera."

Her lips hovered so close that Abbie had no choice. It was either now or never.

Their mouths had barely touched before Abbie clasped her hands upon Joyce's chest and muffled words spilled from her occupied lips.

Oh, wow. Holy shit. It's happening. We're actually kissing! The only reason Abbie could hardly believe it was because she had been dreaming of it for so long – the odds of it ever coming true felt next to impossible. Yet here they were. Here was *Joyce,* her body warm and her lips fire-hot. Their tentative pecks soon transformed to full kisses that drew Abbie's tongue into Joyce's mouth. A few seconds later? *She's touching me. Holy shit, she's grabbing me back!* Those were Joyce's hands making their glorious ascent beneath Abbie's sweater. It had never been enough to dream about kissing and touching this reachable woman through a computer screen. Those fantasies had also included being touched and adored in return. Something Abbie was, unfortunately, not too familiar with in her young life.

She had girlfriends before. She wasn't a virgin. But a "real," long-term thing that included such eager caresses and a desire to be together felt as foreign as being alone on Christmas. *I'm so happy I could cry.*

Ah, shit. A tear actually made its way down her cheek. Abbie covertly brushed it away before pouncing upon Joyce and pinning her down onto the couch.

"Here?" Abbie gasped, legs slipping effortlessly between Joyce's. "Or bed?"

Joyce wrapped both arms around her and pulled her down. "Here first," she purred. "Bed later. It's gonna be a long night, Abs."

Merry Fucking Christmas!

Chapter 10

Joyce remained torn in two different directions. A part of her wanted some time to herself, to reflect upon her feelings and how "right" she could make everything with the woman who had been generous enough to open up her home during a global pandemic.

The other, more numerable parts of her? Wanted to bang. Right here on this couch.

It was either that or wallow in self-pity. *Ever since she asked me about my mother... and I lied.* Joyce had thought about telling the truth, but it would have caused too many problems. Abbie would have fussed over her. Ask, *"Are you sure you want to be here right now?"* or ask her, *"Why didn't you tell me? Holy crap, Joyce, this is a big deal!"* Like Joyce didn't know. Like she didn't want to bury it in her heart right now and forget about it entirely.

It's all in the past. Who cares about my mother's physical death, when I lost her many years ago? Joyce was more interested in making the most of her trip to the coast. There was this beautiful woman who had been making eyes at her for a day. A woman who knew most of Joyce's intimate, dirty secrets, thanks to naughty dates on the computer. *She's already seen my pussy a few dozen times. She might as well know what it feels like tonight.*

Joyce was convinced that this was what was best, not only for her, but Abbie as well. Why make her wait any longer? Joyce would only be there for a few days, and when she returned to Portland? Who knew when she might have the chance to come back. The world was crazy beyond their bubble. *God, don't I know it. This whole year has been crazy.* Every time Joyce thought about it, she got a little heated. Not in the fun, sexy way, either. Frustration.

At how lonely she felt on any given night.

She didn't have to feel lonely tonight. This was her chance to run off and forget about everything. Nothing existed. Not even the rampant thoughts in her head that told her she had once again forgotten how to breathe.

She was finally kissing Abbie. These lips she had been staring at for months were hers to touch in the cozy light of the room. Joyce was free to put her hands around Abbie's cheeks and hold that face there. Long enough to kiss.

More than enough time to find a groove. Because they may have still worn most of their clothing, but that didn't stop them from getting what they wanted *now*. This was seven months of pent-up sexual frustration exploding between them. There could be better lovemaking with more finesse later. Right now, Joyce just...

She just wanted to forget!

"Go on," she whispered, hands clinging to Abbie's sturdy shoulders. "Fuck me. Go for it. Hump me on your couch."

Whatever Abbie thought didn't matter. From the moment she began thrusting against Joyce, to the time she heard those fleeting moans of joy, everything was exactly what Joyce imagined when she drove two hours from Portland in the middle of the damn winter weather.

So why didn't she feel better?

Maybe if she thrust harder, held Abbie closer, or kissed her with more desire, she would feel better. Shadows may dance on the back of her eyelids, and the scent of cheap shampoo may fill her nostrils, but none of those things mattered. It was either have sex or scream into the thundering void of the sea crashing upon itself.

I'm finally kissing you. You're finally kissing me. Those were the thoughts she sent out, hoping Abbie picked up on them.

Instead, Abbie pulled away, her sweater halfway up her torso and her hand wiping something away from her mouth.

"What's wrong?" Joyce propped herself up on the couch. Her hair was mussed and her skin hot, but it wasn't supposed to be like this. "Need to take a break already?"

"I dunno..." Abbie pulled her sweater down and sat back on her feet. "I think I might need to go to the bathroom."

"Oh." Joyce played with her hair while watching Abbie get off the couch. "Get going, then. I'll be waiting for you here."

"Right." Abbie looked like she wanted to say something else, but turned around and skedaddled to the bathroom before a single word fell from her lips.

From the corner of the room, Sammy looked up with a long face and a twitch of her ear. "Is it really that weird?" Joyce asked. "I mean, does she go to the bathroom this much?"

The dog had no answers, of course. And the longer Joyce waited, the more uncomfortable she became in only jeans and her bra. At some point, she felt like she had no choice but to pick up her turtleneck, pull it inside-right, and cling it back to her torso.

Right on time for Abbie to come back.

"Oh..." That wasn't disappointment on Abbie's face. That was... relief? "How about some ice cream? I've got some in the fridge."

Hildred Billings

"Sure," Joyce squeaked. "Got anything with chocolate?"

"Chocolate chip with vanilla?"

"Sounds great."

A smile returned to Abbie's face. She hurried into the kitchen, the sounds of dishes clattering and the freezer opening and closing helping Joyce settle back into the couch.

"How about a silly Christmas movie on TV?" Abbie called from the kitchen.

Joyce had already picked up the remote. "Sounds great."

While this wasn't what she had in mind for the rest of the evening, maybe it was what she needed. Her, the couch, ice cream, and TV...

A girlfriend who could put an arm around her and make her feel at home.

Sounds great in theory. Yet as soon as Joyce had a bowl in her hands and a blanket over her lap, she couldn't help but feel like something was still missing. Everything was there. The picturesque scene between two women, the promise of a nice time together... except Joyce was reticent to fully relax in Abbie's ongoing embrace while they ate ice cream and watched TV for the next two hours.

I'm broken. Joyce didn't know why she thought that, exactly. It was normal to be nervous. Just because they had known each other for so long...

Oh, who was she kidding? She wasn't nervous! She was broken!

***

Abbie couldn't sleep that night. Every time she was about to slip into eternal, dreamlike bliss, she turned over and realized that someone was lying right next to her.

Someone she cared deeply about.

I hope she's okay... Something had been off since dinner. While being flirtatious wasn't unlike her, the way she handled herself in life... well, if this had been online, she would have thought up an excuse to hop off for the evening, and Abbie would have been none the wiser.

Yet this was real life. Joyce couldn't hide what she was feeling inside. She may not want to talk about it, but that was okay. Abbie would wait. Patiently.

She had been waiting for months, after all.

After their impromptu date night on the couch, they went their separate ways to get ready for bed. Abbie had assumed Joyce would sleep in the guest bed that night, even after that suggestion that they sleep together that night. But Abbie was barely five minutes out of the shower, towel wrapped around her body and another patting her hair dry, when she stepped into her room and saw Joyce already curled up in the bed. Sammy sprawled out on Abbie's side of the bed, ready to sleep with them both.

The dog was dragged off the bed. Abbie, however, dropped her towels and crawled in wearing nothing but a long T-shirt.

"Tomorrow's Christmas," she said to Joyce, whose eyelids fluttered open to show she was still awake. "I'll make us pancakes. Hm?"

A wan smile greeted Abbie. "Pancakes sound good. Got any sugar free syrup?"

"Yes. I remember your problems with your teeth. I made sure to get some at the Grocery

Outlet before you got here. I'll even eat it with you."

Joyce chuckled. "You make it sound gross."

"Can't say I've had sugar free syrup in a while..."

"How about you get some sugar right now?" Joyce laid a gentle hand on Abbie's cheek. "A kiss goodnight."

After they allowed their lips to press together, Abbie pulled her head back and asked, "Everything okay with you? Hey, don't want you to feel pressured, but..."

"I'm going through some stuff, sorry." Joyce pulled her covers up toward her chin. "I'll be better tomorrow. It's Christmas, after all. The first I'll celebrate with someone in a long time."

For some reason, although Abbie knew plenty about how lonely Joyce must have been those past few years, it hadn't really sunk in until that moment. "The first one? Wow. I must be pretty special, then. I'm the one who gets to be with you."

"You think that makes you special?" Joyce's tone insinuated she was genuinely surprised by

Abbie's take. "I don't think it makes either of us special. It's only the way life has been."

"I've always had my family," Abbie explained. "Even if we couldn't all be together because of conflicting schedules, there was always someone. I've always had both of my parents. Even last year, when my mother was starting to recover and went into remission, I got to be with her. I just had to prove I got my flu shot," she joked. "Ah, before this year, even if I said I wasn't coming for personal reasons, someone would have tracked me down here and forced me to open presents with them."

"You're very lucky," Joyce said. "I'm the one who should feel special. You've always had that. I'm the one taking you away from them."

"No, you're not." That year kept Abbie from her family. A virus she couldn't see. "Circumstance. And if those circumstances didn't exist, we would have met up a lot sooner."

"We might not have met at all. Would you have gone on a dating website if you weren't stuck in lockdown?"

"Who knows? I honestly can't say." Abbie stroked Joyce's cheek. "All I *can* say is that I'm really glad I met you, and that you're here. Merry Christmas."

They kissed to that.

Chapter 11

When Joyce woke up alone in Abbie's bed on Christmas morning, she wasn't expecting to throw on a sweatshirt and step out to the bathroom to see..

...*This.*

"Merry Christmas!" Abbie popped out of the kitchen, wearing a green "ugly" Christmas sweater and a Santa hat on her head. A string of plastic, bulbous lights – straight from the Dollar Tree, probably – hung around her neck. The spatula in her hand only distracted Joyce long enough before she saw the Hallmark Christmas movie playing on the TV, set to a low volume while Bing Crosby blasted from Abbie's phone in the kitchen. *I never thought I'd have to hear "White Christmas" again in my life.* One of those songs Joyce totally forgot until it played around her. It had been one of her grandmother's favorite singles which, Joyce supposed, wasn't unusual since it was supposedly the bestselling one of all time. *She used to watch it every day when she was sitting at home in a wheelchair, suffering from dementia.* The same dementia that had claimed her daughter fifteen years later.

Great. Now she was thinking of *that,* and she had just got up!

"Me... merry Christmas." Joyce rubbed the sleep from her eyes and continued down the hallway. "I've gotta pee."

"Oh, right!" Abbie swung the spatula through the air as she spoke. "When you're done and dressed, I've got pancakes ready to go! Hope you like blueberries!"

"Ah..." Joyce hesitated in the bathroom doorway. "Not really. Berries upset my stomach, remember?" She wouldn't be sent to the hospital on Christmas, but she might spend part of the morning trapped in the bathroom. Was it worth it for some tarty flavors?

Surprise overcame Abbie's face. "That's right. I remember now. Good thing I haven't actually put in the blueberries yet! Tell you what. I'll make it chocolate chips instead, and I'll put some of the blueberries on top of mine!"

"Sounds great." The mere mention of blueberries made Joyce's gut rumble. "I really gotta go."

A part of her already needed a reprieve from the holiday vomit spewing across Abbie's house. *I thought I could handle it yesterday. Of course there would be decorations. Maybe a cheesy movie. Except I suddenly can't breathe.* Bing Crosby. It had to be Bing Crosby singing "White Christmas" from *Holiday Inn*. Every time Joyce closed her eyes, she saw him. Yet then the movie morphed from *Holiday Inn* to the titular *White Christmas*. 'Cause of course old Hollywood rode that pony into the sunset.

Bing Crosby. Danny Kaye. Rosemary Clooney, and... what was her name? Joyce sat on the toilet, pondering this very thing while the stale scent of a pumpkin air freshener lingered in the room. *Vera-Ellen. That's right.* She had seen those title cards so many times, that she would never forget the name Vera-Ellen.

There the four of them were, dancing and singing together in that derelict lodge in the hopes of making some old general's dreams come true.

I can't believe I remember that much. This was the same woman who could recite every line from *Independence Day* because her mother had worn out so many VHS tapes in the late nineties. When the women in her family found a piece of media they loved, they played it to literal death.

She didn't have to worry about that anymore. They were all gone now. So were the men.

Joyce snuck back into the guest room, where she pulled out a plain gray pullover and a pair of jeans. She brushed her hair in front of the mirror, but didn't bother with makeup. Abbie had seen her plenty without makeup before.

The bags beneath her eyes and the stress clawing at her cheeks shouldn't be new. If there was any day of the year Joyce was allowed to look like crap, it was Christmas, let alone the first Christmas without even a phone call to her mother's nursing home.

Abbie was already plating the pancakes and a plastic-packaged container of freshly cut fruit on the table. She asked Joyce if she wanted coffee or tea before remembering her girlfriend was a tea person. After that, the only real question was if Joyce wanted orange-spice or Earl Gray to go with her pancakes.

Joyce sat down. Bing Crosby was playing on a damned loop. The plates were nothing like the ones they used before. Instead of plain beige porcelain, Joyce looked at giant snowflakes on the edges – and candy-cane shaped pancakes on top.

"It's so exciting to have a reason to use this stuff," Abbie said, hustling out of the kitchen with their tea. "If it were me, I wouldn't bother! So, thanks for being here, I guess." She sat down at the head of the table, adding a bit of cream to her tea. "I don't know what I would do if it were only me and Sammy eating cereal for breakfast on Christmas day."

The dog perked up its head from its giant blue bed in the corner of the room. Joyce grimaced, hoping Abbie hadn't noticed.

"Don't worry about Sammy. She won't beg at the table. Besides, I took her for a long walk at the beach before coming back here to cook breakfast. Did you sleep well?"

"Huh?" Joyce had been staring at the sugar free syrup container. "Oh. Yeah. Slept pretty great, actually." No dreams. The best situation to be in when the world was burning.

"Good! You looked fairly conked out when I got up a couple hours ago. Really didn't want to disturb you. Hope I didn't."

"Don't worry. Until I woke up, I had no idea what was going on out here." Like candy-cane shaped pancakes. *How did she do this? Some kind of mold?* Were the Greywoods really into Christmas? To the point they had a mold for everything? "Didn't you say something about a Zoom call with your parents?"

"Oh, yeah, that's in another hour. We're going to open presents on camera. You don't have to be there if you don't want."

"I don't want to intrude…"

"My parents know you're here. I'm sure they won't mind! Besides, don't you want to open the presents I got you?"

Joyce glanced at the small collection of presents by the tree. "You got me presents?"

"Of course. Why wouldn't I? Didn't you bring me presents? Or are those decoration, huh?"

Joyce shoved a piece of pancake into her mouth before she was compelled to answer. Unfortunately for her, it was a piece with so much syrup wrapped around it, that she almost choked on the fake maple flavor.

"Like I said, I don't want to intrude."

"You can't possibly intrude with my family. They're the types to commandeer your soul and make you one of them before you have the chance to walk away."

Great. Sound like my kind of people. Sometimes, even Joyce surprised herself with how cynical she could sound. "Sounds fun."

She hoped that wasn't dripping with so much sarcasm that Abbie caught on to how unhappy she already was.

I don't want to feel this way... Joyce really didn't think this was going to affect her so much. After all, she was a grown woman who knew how to push down her feelings and do what had to be done. She had spent most of her adult life like that. *You have so much happen to you that you kinda stop feeling anything at all.* She knew it wasn't healthy, but what could she do? Therapy? The waiting lists were a mile long, and Joyce didn't know what she would say to a therapist, anyway. She was simply one of millions of young women who had been orphaned and made alone right before Christmas.

She ventured for a shower after breakfast, although she made sure to offer washing the dishes before she hopped into the bathroom. Abbie insisted that she would take care of the dishes, and that Joyce, "*Should do whatever to make you comfortable.*" Only Joyce didn't know what that was. *A run. I want to go for a run.* The promenade called. With all the carbs she had consumed, she should be good to go for over half an hour. *Run. Run and forget everything that's ever fucked me up.* If Joyce wanted to keep her personal drama away from Abbie's business, that was the best way to do it. Suck it up. Hold it in. Try not to be a bother while everyone else enjoyed their Christmases with their families.

Maybe Joyce would say something about her mother's death tomorrow. It would be more appropriate then.

"...It's a really beautiful day today! Although I read it's supposed to rain later. Go figure." That was Abbie, sitting in front of her coffee table by the Christmas tree. Her laptop was open and a face moved on the screen. "I was hoping to go to the beach later today, but I don't know if that's going to happen now. Sounds as nice to simply stay in here and make a fire to sit before. Hot chocolate. Peppermint. The works!"

"Mind you don't give yourself any cavities with those sweet things." That middle-aged woman's voice was foreign to Joyce's ears. She had come out of the guest room with a more seasonally appropriate outfit on, but she wasn't prepared to meet Abbie's mother quiet yet.

"I brush my teeth after every meal. Promise." Joyce could almost see Abbie crossing her fingers behind her back.

"Hey! Is that her!" A nose was right up in the camera of someone else's laptop. Abbie looked over her shoulder and found her girlfriend tiptoeing behind the couch. *Damnit. There goes my effort to grab my tea without being detected.* "Bring her over here! I want to meet her!"

Abbie gestured for Joyce to come to the living room. "Hey! My mom's on! You want to say hi! For a second?"

Did Joyce really have a choice? She was, after all, staying in the Greywoods' vacation home. Would be awfully rude to turn down the chance to say hello to one of the actual owners. *Not to mention my girlfriend's mother...* It had to happen at some point. While Joyce would prefer any other day except Christmas, well...

her own mother would have said, *"You can wish in one hand and shit in the other and see which one fills up first, honey."* Point well taken.

Joyce slowly approached the back of the couch. Abbie's expectant face asked her to take a look at the camera in the laptop. When Joyce peered over her girlfriend's shoulder, she encountered the worn face of a woman who would have killed Santa Claus himself if it meant her little girl could be there with her on Christmas.

"Hello there, dear! My name's Lois! I'm Abbie's mom!"

Those words came through loud and clear. A little too loud. Never clear enough.

"Mom," Abbie muttered. "She's standing behind me, not on the other side of the house."

"Oh, sorry." Now Lois was whispering. She was also shoving her nostrils toward the camera. A few seconds later, both Joyce and Abbie realized that Lois was walking around her house with her smartphone in her hand. "So nice to finally meet you, Joyce. Abbie's told me so much about you since you met a few years ago. I'm ecstatic that you took the time out of your life to go visit my little girl so she wouldn't be all alone on Christmas."

"Really don't need the guilt trip, Mom."

Joyce leaned over the back of the couch, tea in her hand. "It's a pleasure to meet you, too, Lois. I was surprised when Abbie offered to let me come stay with her, but..."

"But nothing! I raised her to be a very courteous girl! You two just mind your manners, all right? I don't want the neighbors calling me because you two are partying during quarantine."

"The only party we're having, Mom, is when Sammy gets her dinner and goes crazy."

"How *is* Sammy? Where is she? Oh! Here's everyone else! HEY! EVERYONE." The smartphone camera whipped around. When the dust settled and the screen was no longer blurry, Joyce beheld the breadth of Abbie's family aside from her mother. *There's her Dad. There are the twin brothers, their wives, and their school-aged children.* The whole

Greywood clan was there for Christmas, making the most out of their three-house bubble. The kids were decked out in pajamas that suggested they had spent the night at Grandma and Grandpa's so they could enjoy a full Christmas morning experience.

As soon as everyone noticed Lois coming into the room with the phone in her hand, they lifted their hands in greeting to Abbie, who waved back with a squeak in her throat.

"Tony! Dad! Troy! Jessie! Marcella!" When the camera focused on the kids quickly consumed by their curiosity, the naming continued, "William! Kaiden! Annette!" Abbie was about to fuse with her laptop, arms wrapped around it while her cheek pressed into the screen. "Give me your auntie Abbie a hug!"

"Hey!" The loudest voice to overpower everyone else's was a thirty-something man in a black turtleneck and product in his hair. "Who's the lady you got with you, sis? Do we need to come over there and scope her out for you?"

Joyce backed away from the couch. *Thank God they're not here in person.* They were already too loud and too overwhelming for only-child Joyce, who was used to quiet, pensive Christmas mornings that were at most peppered with the 24-hour news channel and the occasional song playing on the radio station. *My family wasn't quiet, per se, but there was never any reason for them to make so much sound.*

"No need to do anything, you big jock," Abbie admonished big brother. "Everybody, this is Joyce. Joyce, this is everybody."

Was all that cheering and shouting for Joyce? Or was that simply the Greywoods' collective response to everything? Joyce couldn't tell now, and she sure as hell couldn't tell as the morning wore on with the winter sun shining and presents collecting on the table.

Oh, my God. These people might classify as animals. Joyce thought that in the nicest way possible, but she was once again grateful that she wasn't actually with the Greywoods that Christmas. If she thought the kids tore into their presents like it was nothing, then the adults were worse! For almost fifteen minutes, there was only the sound of paper tearing and ribbons unfurling, complete with static from Lois's phone. Every so often, one of the kids shrieked in glee, or one of the twin men bellowed that the other owed him five bucks for something or other. Meanwhile, Abbie had no problem following suit. Joyce sat on the far edge of the couch to avoid the paper and bows flying her way. Every time she heard, *"Thanks, Mom!"* it was followed up with, *"Whoa! Is this what I think it is?"* To her credit, she was excited to share everything with her girlfriend, who gave a glance to whatever was in Abbie's hand at the moment and otherwise distracted herself with tea that had long gone cold.

Bing Crosby was still playing in the background. On repeat.

"Is that 'White Christmas' I hear?" Lois exclaimed ten minutes into the unwrapping frenzy. "Oh, I love that song!"

"That's part of the reason I'm playing it. Are you guys gonna watch the movie later?"

"We do every year! Hey, we should watch it together. It's on Netflix this time!"

"Awesome!" Abbie turned to Joyce. "You don't mind if we watch *White Christmas*, do you? It's sort of a family tradition."

"Here I thought you would tell me it's *Meet Me in St. Louis*."

Abbie gasped. "That was my favorite movie as a kid! Man, I loved so many of those classic films."

Lois laughed over the camera. "Abbie's first loves were Judy Garland and Audrey Hepburn. You ask me, I knew she was gay from the time she was seven years old and watching *Roman Holiday* with her eyes all big every time Audrey came on the screen."

Abbie blushed. "She was *really* pretty. I wished my hair was as dark as hers instead of this garbled color I've got." She grabbed a chunk of her dirty blond hair, as if she had anything to be disappointed about. "You know, like your hair, Joy. You've got a gorgeous hair color!"

"It's true!" Lois chimed in. "It looks very soft and silky. How do you get it that way?"

"Uh, I wash and brush it..."

"It's no wonder that our daughter is so enamored with you, sweetie. You are a gorgeous young woman, and we welcome you to the family."

Lois panned the camera over the destructive scene in her own family. Paper covered the floor. Kids in footed pajamas hurled themselves over furniture while new toys flew in their hands. One of the brothers helped adjust his wife's Ugly Sweater collar. Dwayne the dad marched out of the kitchen, demanding to know who had stuck their finger in that afternoon's ham that was about to go into the oven. When one of the little boys giggled so hard that he caught Dwayne's attention, Lois lowered the camera and suggested that her grandson help grandpa with the ham since he "clearly liked it so much."

"Maybe next year you can be here with us, Joyce." Lois's sweet demeanor was turned back on when she readdressed both Joyce and Abbie. "It's not the same without our darling daughter here. I know you did what you thought you had to, Abs, but we *miss* you!"

Abbie wiped something from her eye. "I miss you guys, too. Don't worry, though. Joyce being here means I'm not alone this Christmas."

That statement made Joyce sit back again. *I didn't realize this visit really meant so much to her.* Maybe Abbie was more like Joyce than initially thought. *Putting on a bright, smiling face. Or in my case, a neutral face. Either way, we're keeping everyone around us happy while we hold all our of emotions inside. Super healthy.*

She should tell Abbie about what had happened. Soon.

Not now. Not while she was having a moment with her family.

"I wish we were there on the beach with you right now, honey." That was one of the last things Lois said before they finally ended the call a little after noon. "It's all I've been able to think about this year. I really, really hope next year is better."

She was crying, although she attempted to keep the camera away from her face. Joyce respectfully kept to her end of the couch while

Abbie said her farewell to her mother, who was soon nothing more than a recent memory through the internet.

"Man..." Abbie wiped more tears from her face. After she sucked something up her nose, she said, "Don't know why I'm crying a bit. Not like I'm never going to see her again."

"You said it was going to be hard this year, after what happened to her *last* year."

"Guess so. Seeing everyone having a nice Christmas together and I can't be there..."

Abbie closed her laptop lid. She looked like she was about to get up – instead, she doubled-over, face toward her lap and arms stretching before her. *It's like she's trying to reach her family through the laptop.*

Joyce was *this* close to scooting over and seeing if her girlfriend needed reassurance. Yet as she was about to touch her, Abbie jerked up, smile back on her face.

"You still have some presents to open!" She tossed aside the wrapping paper that had amassed on the coffee table and the floor between it and the couch. There, beneath a couple of bows that had no business being there, were three presents marked for Joyce.

"Oh, should we exchange presents now?" For someone who had taken a lot of care picking out her presents for Abbie, she could no longer remember what she had bought the woman who had offered her much. "All right."

"Wait. While you do that, I've got something to bring out from the kitchen."

What now? With a present in her lap, Joyce watched Abbie return to the kitchen, skip no longer in her step. At least someone had finally turned off Bing Crosby.

...Only to replace it with Mariah Carey.

"I draw the line!" Joyce shouted over her shoulder. "I can't do it!"

The song stopped on Abbie's phone. "Sorry! Trying to make it festive! Hey, how about we watch *White Christmas* while we open our presents? Mom said it was on Netflix."

"Sure," Joyce said through clenched teeth. "Love to. Haven't seen it in forever."

A platter of store-bought Christmas cookies appeared on the coffee table. Abbie moved her laptop to another chair before sitting down on the couch. Sure enough, here came the Netflix loading screen on the TV. *T-Minus to when Bing Crosby is singing to me again.*

"God, I love these kinds of movies." Abbie's hands were around her face. Sammy got up from her bed and decided to join them on the couch. "There's something so magical about these old movies, you know? When I was a kid, I wanted to believe that every few minutes would be someone breaking out into song."

Joyce bit her lip. "Yeah... my grandma used to watch these all the time. Though I definitely preferred these to the John Wayne naval flicks she used to watch, too."

"Was this the same grandma with the attic full of old Harlequin books?"

"The very same. She would tell everyone to look away if someone was kissing in an old movie, but as soon as we closed our eyes, she pulled out a bodice-ripper from her purse and flipped through the pages."

Abbie giggled. The title card for *White Christmas* appeared on the screen. Once she saw Beverly Clooney's name, Joyce looked away.

"I wish I could meet your family. Oh, do you want to call your mom today and wish her a Merry Christmas?"

Joyce was blindsided by that comment. To the point she watched Bing and Danny, dressed for WWII, gather around to sing a song for the superior officer. "No, I don't think that's a good idea. It will upset her," Joyce lied.

"Oh. That's right. Sorry I brought it up." Abbie sighed. "Here I am shoving my family in your face, and I can't even meet yours. But I can do this." She handed a slim present to her girlfriend, who had already forgotten they were exchanging presents. "Merry Christmas, hon. I hope this isn't our only one."

Joyce couldn't stay upset. As soon as she saw that placid look on Abbie's face, everything was better again.

Although the shape of the box suggested it was jewelry of some kind, Joyce was still surprised to see the gold chain and her name spelled out in diamond-studded letters.

"Whoa." She lifted the small necklace to the light. "Thank you. It's beautiful."

"Really? I was worried it wasn't original enough. There's this lady who often comes into my shop, and she makes these kinds of necklaces for people. Put in an order for it all the way back in October." That mischievous grin on Abbie's face could only mean one thing. "She had no idea it was for my girlfriend. Tee fucking hee!"

There it was. Abbie got a little kick out of pulling the homosexual wool over some of her neighbors' eyes, huh? Joyce could help with that. She'd start by leaning in and kissing her girlfriend on the lips – in front of the drawn curtains and everything!

"I'm glad you like it," Abbie sheepishly whispered when she pulled away. "You have such a beautiful name, Joyce. I like how it makes me think of this festive time of year. Honestly, having you here... it's a dream come true."

Joyce lifted the necklace against her chest and closed the clasp around her neck. The golden and diamond JOYCE settled nicely upon her sweater. How had Abbie guessed the right chain length? Or was it a fluke?

"My mom picked my name because she really loved Christmas. It was either Joyce or Holly." A wan smile lifted up the corners of Joyce's mouth, but she wouldn't call it a *real* smile. "Did I ever tell you the story about my mom and the local Jehovah's Witness ladies?"

"I don't recall."

"I must have mentioned something about how they often came around. About once a month. I mean, they kept coming because my mom always invited them in to talk. I think she liked the company, especially after I had gone off to college and she became estranged from what was left of my family." Was this before or after her father died? Must have been before... "She said they could stay as long as they didn't 'spout off' about no birthdays and no Christmas. She made it damn clear that she didn't worship her Christmas tree, and it was one of the only things that made her happy after her own mother died."

"Except you were edgy Joyce back then, so you thought Christmas trees were stupid."

Joyce laughed. "How could you guess?"

"Because I remember this story now. You said your mother was seriously hurt when you said the tinsel looked super tacky."

"It was also dangerous for the cats! If any of our cats got their mouths on the tinsel, boom!" Joyce mimicked what it might look like if a kitten's stomach blew up.

Only Abbie would match that with uproarious laughter. "I know! What is it with moms and wanting to deck everything out in tinsel? We didn't have cats when we finally broke my mom of the habit, but it was almost worst... we had toddlers running around the house! The kind of toddlers that put *everything* in their mouths!

Joyce picked a gift up from the table and handed it to her girlfriend. "Your turn. I want to see your big smile when you see what I've got you."

She soon got her wish. Good. Because Joyce would give anything for the world to take away the painful Christmas memories festering in the back of her mind.

Chapter 12

For most of the day, Joyce managed to keep her shit together. It helped that there was a distraction around every corner. Like Abbie nodding off to sleep during *White Christmas,* allowing Joyce to lean back in the sofa and scroll through her phone instead of paying attention to a movie that made her think of her mother and grandmother every time she looked Bing Crosby in the face.

Then Abbie snorted herself awake and exclaimed it was time for *Meet Me in St. Louis.*

"Did you know that the lyrics were a little different in 'Have Yourself a Merry Christmas?'" she asked, while Judy sang to

Margaret O'Brien. "In the original verse, they made it sound like everyone could be dead next year. Judy complained about it because she didn't want to sing such depressing lyrics to a little kid. So, we got a much better version."

This was, in fact, a tidbit that Joyce had heard before. "In a way, the guy who wrote it wasn't too far off. For a lot of people, it is their last Christmas, whether they know it or not."

Abbie cocked her head. "Yeah. Guess so."

Joyce stood up from the couch. She had almost suggested they go for a walk outside, but the sky had darkened and dumped some rain onto the pavement long before they finished unwrapping their presents and cleaning up the paper left on the floor. Sammy got her exercise from attacking the bows and ribbons that unearthed themselves from the piles of papers Abbie had somehow amassed even without her family present that year.

Ignoring everything around Joyce was becoming increasingly difficult.

The songs. The movies. The pristine tree with the lovely presents beneath the tree. Fun pancakes and Christmas cookies. Abbie's scratchy sweater that served no purpose other than to look kitschy and ridiculous. Until that afternoon, Joyce hadn't pinpointed why she felt the way she did.

I'm stressed the hell out. She had come here to escape the memories of her mother and the family she no longer had that Christmas, arguably one of the worst times of the year for newly-orphaned children. Or, if her own mother had been anyone to go by, for anyone who intimately knew the pains of grief for several years.

Grief wasn't supposed to be like this for Joyce, though. She had been through it already. Multiple times. She knew what it entailed and how she would feel. Or *should* feel.

She also knew how else she should feel. *Content. Happy. Grateful that Abbie is here and has opened her home to me during such uncertain times.* Joyce had not come to Seaside to be a huge bummer in her girlfriend's life. If anything, she was here to forget the crap. Get away from the hell. Forget anything that made her want to scream into her pillow deep into the night.

Abbie didn't deserve sad, cranky Joyce. Of course, reminding herself that only made Joyce feel worse. She was bringing down the mood. Soon, Abbie would resent having invited her here. *"Why did I invite you if this is how you're going to act? Don't you know I love Christmas? I gave up Christmas with my own family for you!"* That's what Joyce imagined her saying as soon as Abbie caught on to the mood in the room.

Because the intrusive thoughts about everything else weren't bad enough. Now Joyce had to have them about how much Abbie probably resented her. Nothing happened yet!

"Everything okay?" Abbie asked from the couch. "I could put on another movie if you want."

Crap. She's on to me. Joyce tacked on a fake smile before turning around and facing the woman who immediately saw through it. "Everything's great!" *God damnit, Joyce, dial it back a bit!* What was she supposed to do, though? She only had two speeds! Over-the-top happy girlfriend and giant black hole of despair! "I *love* this movie. Judy Garland. What a babe, right?"

Both of Abbie's eyebrows traveled up her head. "I think you had too much tea. I'm gonna give you decaf from now on."

The dog dragged itself from the couch and stood before Joyce, tail wagging in anticipation. "What's with her?" Joyce asked.

"Oh, you're standing near the front door, so she thinks you want to take her for a walk." Abbie glanced at the rain pouring outside. "Ugh. Not right now, Sam. Maybe later when we don't have a choice."

"Do you really take her out for walks in the pouring rain?"

"What is the alternative, huh? Let her crap on my floor? When the weather is dreadful, I stand in the yard and let her do business there. It's a trade-off few dogs can understand."

"I see. I'm... gonna go to the bathroom."

"You sure you okay?" Abbie called after her. "You're going to the bathroom a lot."

"Maybe I really gotta go!" Joyce slammed the door behind her before she had to answer any further questions. Finally, she had a reprieve. *Not sure what for. To get away from old movies? To sit on the toilet and scroll through my phone?* God, that would be toxic. Everything on her phone would be nothing but warm, Christmas memories with family and big dinners meant to settle in the stomach for days to come. While Joyce wouldn't begrudge any happiness people could find – let alone in that year, of all years – she reserved the right to not have to see it. If there were a way to curate a social media that was nothing but generic cat pictures, she would snap her fingers and make it happen right now.

I... want... I don't know.

Her elbows dug into her thighs as she masked her face with her hands. For some reason, she couldn't breathe. No matter how much she drew in a breath or focused on letting the air roll through her body, someone – or something – was choking her throat and enticing her to fall onto the bathroom floor.

"Joyce?" Abbie lightly knocked on the door. "You okay?"

No. Joyce hadn't been okay in a long time. She honestly couldn't remember the last time she felt *good.*

Maybe... talking to Abbie on the computer. That wasn't to say she couldn't appreciate Abbie in real life, too. Yet it was different, wasn't it? Like a social media feed, it was easier to curate a specific experience when she only knew someone through a computer screen. She could turn off a camera or a mic. Walk out of the room. Have to suddenly do something else and cut the call short. Every date that went on for hours was a great memory, because Joyce had the power to pull the plug whenever she wanted.

Not like real life, where everything came in its own package. She had to unwrap the whole thing. She couldn't ignore one aspect of a relationship in favor for only the things she liked.

The door eased open. Joyce had forgotten to lock it.

"I'm not looking, promise." Abbie's blond scalp appeared in the sliver of doorway. "Making sure you're okay. Something seems really off with you."

Joyce had half a mind to tell her to bugger off, but what was the point? She was cornered. Had. Found out.

"It's fine. I'm not going to the bathroom." Joyce sniffed. *Allergies. Congestion. That's all.* She wasn't crying. "Need a few minutes to myself."

"Sorry if I'm coming off as overbearing..." The door opened more. Abbie had a cookie in her hand. "Want some sugar?"

Joyce shook her head. "No."

"Oh. Okay." The door slightly closed again. "Do you want to talk about it?"

"No."

"Okay." The door was fully closed.

God, this is so embarrassing. No getting out of this now. Even if Joyce went back out there, chattering about this and that, Abbie would *know* something was wrong. Yet how was Joyce supposed to put it into words? How could she make requests without hurting Abbie's feelings. *We may be girlfriends, but in the end, we barely know each other.* This was a terrible idea. Coming to Seaside during a pandemic to meet a woman she had only known online for a few months. What had Joyce been thinking?

When she finally walked back out into the living room, she was met with a whole plate of cookies in her face.

"You sure you don't want any?" Although Abbie's grin was genuine, everything about her demeanor smacked Joyce right in the face.

"I'm sure," she said through clenched teeth. "Honestly, I need a break from 'Christmas' for about an hour or so."

"A break from Christmas?" Incredulous, Abbie lowered her plate of sugary cookies. "You mean that?"

Joyce sighed. "I know this comes as a shock to some people, but not everyone *likes* Christmas! There's such a thing as too much of a good thing."

Abbie was either shocked or hurt – perhaps, she was both. For every part of Joyce that wanted to break down and apologize for how she was acting, there was another screaming at her to get the hell out of there. *I need some time to myself.* That's how she rationalized it as she grabbed her jacket off the coat rack and flung open the front door to meet a smattering of sideways rain hitting the street.

"Joyce!" Abbie followed her as far as the door. Behind her, Sammy barked in excitement. It took all of Abbie's attention to keep her dog from running outside without a leash. "Where are you going?"

"For a walk!" Joyce tightened the jacket around her body and flung the hood over her head. She didn't mind the rain. She swore it. "I need to get away from this crap, okay?"

"Are you..." Abbie was barely audible, now that Joyce was by the gate, rain prickling against her jacket. "Are you coming back?"

What a stupid question! Of course Joyce was coming back!

But she didn't say that as she slammed open the gate and stomped out onto the empty street. The wind blew harder than she anticipated, but she stood steady and marched toward the first intersection that was in her periphery vision.

Already, her anger was vindicated. It was much easier to cry in the rain, after all. Nobody could tell that's why her face was all wet.

Chapter 13

The thing about long, empty beaches? There was nowhere to sit.

Joyce stood before the surf, hands in her pockets and seafoam tickling the tips of her boots. The cold already pierced her jacket and the hair covering her ears. What was the extra sting of the freezing cold Pacific Ocean to her?

She wouldn't mind sitting down. This was a woman who had made it to the beach in record time, her mind burning hot with memories of a family that no longer existed and the crass, unbridled feeling of being *the last*. The wet sand wasn't too hard to walk on, but her calves ached. Her ankles throbbed. Her heart beat so hard from the adrenaline coursing through her that the last bit of rationalization in her head told her to sit the hell down before she hurt herself. Or had a stroke.

I don't care. I don't care if God strikes me dead here and I am carried away in the tide. Big words for a woman who was hydrophobic enough to occasionally get a panic attack looking at the ocean. Drowning was always one of her biggest fears. *Besides, pretty big of me to think that God cares enough to spend that much time on me.* God didn't go around smiting ungrateful, grieving women standing on some forgotten beach on Christmas. If He existed, He was too busy punishing people who had committed heinous crimes. *Like "Law & Order" level of heinous.* Not some thirty-year-old who was the last of her family.

She would like to sit down.

The only place to properly sit was on one of the several swing sets, but they all seemed so far away. So she stood there in front of the waves, hands in pockets, hood constantly flying off her head, eyes wide open and rain and spray stinging her face. She had the beach to herself. Just her, the rolling waves, and the squawking seagulls looking for one last bite to eat.

And a dog sniffing at her feet.

Joyce didn't turn around. Instead, she bowed her head, telling herself to get the tears out now before she was further embarrassed.

She didn't know how long she stood there like that. Silent. Mind empty. Tears streaming down her face as she inhaled and curled her hands into fists within her pockets. Sammy barked at her once before running off again. The little dog footprints were left in the wet sand. The next wave to roll in couldn't even cover it up.

If I walked away right now, my footprints would be left behind, too. Eventually, they would disappear – but if anyone else went for a walk that day, they would see the spot where Joyce Stewart stood and contemplated the state of her life.

Was that how Abbie found her? Followed her footprints once she reached the beach and realized there was no one else there?

Joyce didn't know how long she continued to stand there. The rumbling groans of the tumultuous ocean were the only things keeping her sane in those cosmically arcane seconds. They crashed in time with her beating heart – or, perhaps, it was her heart matching the rhythm of the erratically synced waves as they came to her from another land.

The ocean didn't care. The sea was a neutral witness who neither judged nor offered meaningful support. Was that why Joyce always had a little resentment for it? Back when she was a child, the ocean was scary. It would snatch her off the beach, haunting her dreams until she understood the power it possessed. In real life, though? It didn't mean to take her. It hadn't *meant* to take any of the people it did. When everyone in Joyce's hometown said "respect the ocean" and "don't turn your back on the ocean" it was because of the indiscriminate nature of nature's most bountiful body.

For the first time in her life, Joyce understood the appeal of this place. The ocean was a great equalizer. No matter your politics, your history, or your culture, you were as equally welcomed as the person standing behind you.

Suppose I should go ahead and face her now. Even so, Joyce's head remained bowed as she turned toward Abbie, who had stood a decent distance behind her that whole time.

Abbie said nothing. Joyce sniffed up however many tears it took for her to be a coherent human being again.

"I'm sorry." Her voice was lost on the wind and in the thunder of the ocean. Sand squished beneath her feet when she took a step forward. "I'm a big fucking mess."

Sammy danced around Abbie's legs. After the third bark that echoed down the beach, Abbie picked up the stick that was at her feet and chucked it as far as she could. Sammy took off, oblivious to the woes of humans.

"You wanna talk about it?" Abbie asked. "Or do you wanna stand here on the beach, on Christmas Day, and cry?"

"That one."

Joyce felt a little better when she beheld Abbie's small smile. They continued to stand in silence, the only sounds the wagging of the dog's tail and the surf curling around Joyce's feet. *Never turn your back on the ocean. Yet that's the very thing I've done.*

Eventually, though, Joyce would have to announce the truth. The one she had kept locked away in her heart for the past few months.

"My mom died."

The collected demeanor fell from Abbie's face. "What? When?"

Joyce bit her salty lip. "A little while ago. Sometime after Thanksgiving."

Abbie took two steps forward. Sammy saw it as her sign that they were going to play again, but was rebuffed when Abbie ignored her in favor of Joyce. "Why didn't you tell me?"

Although she knew that was the first thing Abbie would say, Joyce was still frustrated to hear it. "When would have been a good time, huh? Whenever I talked to you, I wanted to escape for a little while. Forget my stifling job and how I'd been locked up in my apartment for seven fucking months. Why would I bring up something that was always inevitable?" She pulled her phone out of her pocket. Immediately, the rain splattered against the screen. "What, was I supposed to text you and say, '*My estranged aunt left me a voicemail saying my mom died?*'"

"A *voicemail?*" Abbie lunged forward. Was she about to knock the cursed phone from Joyce's hand? *It doesn't work that way. The voicemail is still on there.* Forever locked in the annals of Joyce's data. "Are you kidding me? She left you a fucking *voicemail?*"

"I kept thinking it could be worse. Could have been a text. Suppose you would have wanted me to forward you that, huh?"

"*Yes!*" Abbie's arms leaped into the air. Her sweatshirt bunched around her chest. Her long, blond hair was browner in the dull light of Christmas Day in Seaside. "Sort of a big deal, isn't it? Your mom died! Why wouldn't you tell me? Why wouldn't your own girlfriend want to know?" Abbie took a step back before she reached Joyce's personal space. "Wait. Do you not think of me as your real girlfriend because we only knew each other online? Was I only an 'escape' for you for all those months?"

"That's not fair," Joyce shot back. "That's not what it was like at all! You don't get to make this all about you right now!"

More tears came to Joyce's eyes. Wiping them away with the bottom of her hand was filled with more frustration than she would care to admit. *I can't believe it. What a time to cry!* Couldn't she believe it, though? She was so damn emotional. Even when she promised herself she had shut down a majority of her feelings, they still came crawling back like little parasites, prepared to infect her rational mind that constantly told her, "*You can't control any of this, so accept it. Shit happens. You move on. You remember that, right, Joyce? Shit. Happens.*"

"My mom died..." She repeated, the tears she had wiped away already returning. "My mom died..." The dam was broken. Both hands were in her eyes, desperately attempting to hide her emotional shame. "I'm never going to see my mom again!"

There it was. It hurt more than the actual thought of her mom dying. *She's been dead a long time. The woman who was my mother... she died.* There was the occasional visit. Chats on the phone. Updates with pictures. The very last gift Joyce received was the previous Christmas, when a manila envelope containing a finger painting showed up at her doorstep. The picture was utter nonsense. Just a mishmash of melded colors, like a preschooler discovering color theory for the first time. Yet the handwritten note included in the envelope carried the words of the memory care facility's manager. *"Your mother was having a good day when she painted this. You know she never wanted to take part in our activities. But today, she did. When she finished, she looked right at the nurse and said, 'I want my daughter to have this.'"*

No more of that. There would never be another gift, another whispered word, or another feeble, bony hug again.

No hope. The hope was all gone.

Although Joyce didn't collapse onto the sand, she covered her face in a futile attempt to hold back her keening. Anyone standing on the other end of Seaside's empty beach would have thought they were haunted by a Christmas banshee come to haunt the town.

"I want my mom!" Joyce cried between her gasping breaths. "I want my family!" All she had to do was open her eyes and remember the days she visited the beach with her parents. Her father digging for agates before suggesting they climb upon slippery rocks and wondering why nobody would follow. Her mother complaining about the sand and the sun beating down upon them. Even Joyce complained, since she hated the smell of the sea air she had lived next to for most of her young life.

Truly, though, the main thing she had been thinking for many days finally reared its ugly head – right inside her mouth.

"I wish I were dead like them!"

That was the hardest thing to even admit to herself. Joyce wasn't suicidal. Not *really*. She didn't actually plan out how she would do the deed – besides, as her mother always said, "*I'm too chickenshit to go through with that, anyway.*" Joyce's curiosity about the future overruled everything else.

Yet that didn't stop some of the more intrusive thoughts that had infiltrated her head that whole year, starting back when visits to the public and even going for a stroll through Target became a thing of the distant past. When Joyce was trapped in her room, with her own head, it was inevitable.

"*I don't want to be alive anymore. I want to not exist. There is no point to anything. Everyone is gone. I don't do anything that matters. It's just me. I'm the only one with the memories.*"

If she could bargain with God for anything in the world, it wouldn't be to bring her mother back. That ship had long sailed. No. Joyce would beg Him to take away her memories of childhood. The good. The bad. The mundanely neutral. Because every memory was tainted now. Even if she remembered a pleasant story about candlelit board games after the power went out, all she recalled immediately after was *they're all dead now. I'll never play board games with them again.*

Wasn't it too much to bear for a woman barely in her thirties? Someone who had no family of her own yet? No support network? Nobody but the faces on the screen, and the words the occasional kind stranger typed when she vented in a Reddit thread? It was too much. During a year when the bad news continued to pile on, realizing that she would never see her mother again – even in a volatile, vulnerable, decaying state – was harder than anything else.

I want my mommy...

The woman who had wanted her so badly that she endured three miscarriages before dumping her first husband and finding a man who, in her words, "could make a baby stick." The woman who was so worried that her daughter was born into a *too* isolating world and worked three jobs to send her to daycare for the sole purpose of socializing with children her age. A mom who could never believe "someone so smart came out of *me*," when Joyce brought home straight As and the praise of her teachers. Her mother was this close to pulling the plug on the internet when Joyce discovered it, but the Photoshop doodles and the websites built after school had awed Joyce's mother so much that she went out of her way to buy more programs and pay for one-shot classes, back when those weren't easy to come by. *She was my biggest cheerleader. My best friend. She told me things she never even told her husbands.* The baby that was buried in Oklahoma. The fears of dying alone. How desperately she missed her own mommy and daddy, and how every Christmas was like someone sitting on her heart. Joyce understood those things now. The constant loss, the grief, and the looking forward for anything, *anything* to make it easier to bear.

It had been so long since Joyce actually had her mother, though, that she often forgot what it was like to have that relationship. When she did remember? It was like someone was sitting on her chest, digging to get to her heart.

"I don't really mean that." Those were the first words Joyce said when she realized how Abbie looked. *Fearful. Frightened. Furious.* In the end, they all meant the same thing. "I don't want to actually be dead. I... don't want to be alive right now." She wanted to take the world's longest nap. One day she could reawaken, a new, healthier woman ready to take on the rest of her life. Right now, though? Naptime.

"I'm glad you don't actually want to die." Abbie came a little closer, her bottom lip shaking and her pale gray eyes wide and glistening. "Because I would miss you. You're the biggest shining light of this shitastic year."

Joyce sniffed up the one thing clogging up her nose. "Really? Even after I've acted like such a brat on your Christmas?"

"Who says you're a brat? Your mom just fucking died! You can be as bratty as you damn well please!" Abbie couldn't hold back her limbs any longer. She flung them around Joyce, squeezing her in a tight embrace that knocked the wind out of her. "It's not *my* Christmas, either." Was Abbie crying, too? Joyce could hardly believe it as she slowly wrapped her arms back around the woman who had followed her all the way to the beach on such a blustery, wet day. "It's our Christmas, silly. I wanted to make it special for you. I thought..." Abbie pulled away, sniffing. Her cheeks were crimson red, but the rest of her face completely washed out. "I was so happy to have a reason to celebrate Christmas. For me, it's all about having at least one person to enjoy it with. Someone who is *family*. Christ, Joyce, you're my family! Why do you think I'm so excited?" Before Joyce could break through how agog she was that she was *family*, Abbie continued, "I had no idea this was so painful for you."

"I... I didn't either, I guess."

Abbie looked down at her feet. The ones sniffed by a dog and occasionally touched by the waves as the tide changed its plans. "Meanwhile, I picked up that something was off with you, but instead of thinking of what you might be going through, I kept pushing what made *me* happy. I guess I thought you were nervous about meeting me after being cooped up for so long. I never thought..." She brushed her hair away from her face, but the wind blew it right back. "Never thought you might be having such intense emotions this time of the year. Never mind with news like *that*."

"Yeah... I'm sorry I kept it from you."

"Hey, it's not my place to demand stuff like that. You tell people when you need to. You're the only one who knows how it feels!"

That was part of the problem. Joyce was so alone in her feelings. Even when she occasionally perused "grief support" forums and subreddits, she often came up against this giant gape between "other people's experiences" and her own. Few could relate to the feeling of insurmountable loss at such a young age – and those who could, often felt it in a very different way. Simply talking about it and watching empathetic faces nod along wasn't the same as someone looking her in the eye and saying, "*I know. You're not alone.*"

She looked into Abbie's eyes now, although the sea air stung and her lungs were full of the sort of breaths that begged her to reassess her life. Abbie might not have any idea what it was like to lose her family like Joyce did, but she had brushed against the prospect of death. That alone spiked fear, grief, and resentment into a woman's body.

Abbie may not have known, but she cared. Wasn't what Joyce needed the most a caring person in her corner? Someone to hold her close, tell her she was worthy of knowing, and offer to build a life with her?

Maybe it was too soon to talk about *that,* but Joyce knew one thing when she looked in those sea gray eyes.

She loves me.

"I love you," Abbie soon blurted. Joyce almost laughed. *Don't! Hold it in! She'll think you're laughing about something else and get hurt!* Instead, Joyce smiled, the disbelief that anyone could love a grieving mess like her hitting harder than the dropping temperature of the beach.

It was getting close to sunset, wasn't it?

"I don't know why I said that." Abbie slapped her fingers over her mouth. "We barely know each other, right? I mean, like seven months of online dating is actually only like two months in real life. Or so I'm guessing."

Joyce suffered another wan smile. "I love you, too. I'm so grateful for you, Abbie."

The relief on Abbie's face was palpable enough to draw Joyce into her wet but warm embrace. Sammy danced around them, barking and prancing upon the sand. Abbie kicked the stick to give the dog something to do, but all the couple of women standing on the beach wanted was to kiss and make up on Christmas Day.

"I love you," Abbie said. "I want you to be happy. I want you to have a great Christmas!"

Joyce sighed, albeit with a smile. "Right now I'll take having a decent Christmas."

"How about before we go back," a finger ran down the length of Joyce's face, inciting her to close her eyes and take a restorative breath, "you yell out some of the pain you're feeling inside? Fresh start for the rest of Christmas."

Joyce pulled her head back. "Yell out?"

"Sure! This is the beach!" Abbie opened her arms wide, as if she could encompass the whole beach within her arms. "Nobody will hear you! If they do, they think it's the waves. No better time than now, either! Hey, sometimes I do it. I come down here when there's nobody else around and yell at the ocean. Feels pretty great. You should try it right now."

"Um..." Joyce slowly turned toward the waves. They looked the same as they had a few minutes before – white caps among the gray, gulls swooping low, and a small sliver of sunlight streaming through the thick gray clouds. Only now she realized her voice, her pain, and her grief would echo across that churning sea until there was no one left to hear.

No one except, perhaps, her mother.

"Go on," Abbie urged. "Let it out! Exhaust yourself!"

Joyce didn't know why she suddenly experienced stage fright. Only ten minutes ago, she was perfectly fine with unleashing her anger upon the beach. Now? Her small audience of one made her self-conscious. Besides! She had professed her love to the woman she had been dating for the past few months! And was told she was loved in return! How could she "unleash" anything now?

"It's bullshit," she said. "This year of all years." Her voice grew a little higher. "Why should I have to go through so much shit in such little time? My mother fucking died!" Here came a few tears again. At least now she had the power to scream at the ocean.

Scream she did.

"Fuck! This! Shit!" Her fists hit her thighs. Her jacket dropped around her arms. "Fuck dealing with this shit! I'm fucking tired!"

Her voice rode the wind. Where it petered out? She had no way to know. Joyce was free to unclench her fists, though, Release the tension. Give way to the undulations of the water coming closer and closer to the shoreline.

"How about we go home?" Abbie's hand appeared on Joyce's shoulder. "I'll make us a fire. We'll do whatever you want after that."

Joyce leaned into Abbie's oncoming embrace. "I can think of one movie I'd like to watch. It's nothing like yours, though."

"You mean it's not Judy or Bing?"

They turned around, arm still on Joyce's shoulder as they approached the promenade. "More like Chevy Chase having a mental breakdown because the tree has too much sap."

"Ah, yes. The ol' Griswold clan kidnapping each other and pumping sewage into the gutter." Abbie removed her arm. "Did you know that *Griswold* actually means grey wood? Some of my ancestors must have had that name. Rather glad they changed it, considering what National Lampoon did to it."

Joyce chuckled. "It was my family's favorite movie every year."

"Hey, like I said. We'll do whatever you want."

Joyce glanced at the swing set they were about to pass. "How about we have a seat?"

It took Abbie a few seconds to get her girlfriend's gist, but the opportunity was not lost on her face. "How about *you* have a seat, and I'll push you."

Joy lit up on Joyce's face. "Not too hard, okay? I'm not seven anymore. I'm not actually looking to fly."

Joyce rushed to the swing set with Abbie right behind her. She looped her arms around the chains the moment her butt met the plastic seat. Soon, her hair was floating behind her, boots kicking out and shrieks of laughter bouncing across the rumbling ocean waves.

Every time she swung back, Abbie's hand was there to push her again. Knowing that there was always someone to have her back finally allowed a large smile of Christmas cheer to overcome Joyce's frozen face.

Chapter 14

The fire crackled as Abbie fed it another log. She didn't often use the fireplace, but in front of Joyce? She would look like the log fire pro her own father was.

She adjusted the grate before retracting her hand. A sigh rippled down her chest. When she stood up again, she realized that Joyce had been watching her the whole time.

Man, she's still so beautiful. She only thought "still" because it had been a long day with the new love of her life. Finding out that Joyce's mother had recently died was both shocking and... a bit of a relief, really. Yet the only thing that truly bothered Abbie was the idea that she was too precarious to share such news with, as if the threat to her *own* Christmas meant she couldn't handle some bad news. Didn't she want Joyce to trust her? To see her as someone to come to when things were tough? Painful? *Direly unforgettable.* Yet Abbie couldn't get hung up on that. Not when those big, hazel eyes looked back at her, while pink, pursed lips blew on the steam of Joyce's hot tea and a blanket wrapped around her legs.

The couch had never looked so cozy. While Joyce blew on her tea and watched Abbie tend the fire, she tucked her hair behind her ear. That big and baggy white sweater invited Abbie to come sit down and snuggle close. Yet she remained a respectful distance away, the fire warming her backside.

"What is it?" Joyce asked.

"Nothing," Abbie was a little too quick to say. "Thinking about stuff."

"You want to come join me on the couch?"

"Actually," Abbie sat down on the carpet before the fireplace, legs crossing and hands hitting her knees. "Why don't you come down here and join me? Much warmer directly in front of the fire."

"Oh." Joyce placed her mug on the table by the couch, but wasn't in a hurry to whip the blanket off her lap. "Sure. I've... well, I've never actually sat before a fire like that one before. We always had a wood stove when I was a kid. The only time you saw the fire was when you fed it more wood."

Abbie spotted the carpet next to her. "Come on down and have a seat. There's plenty of room. Plenty safe, too."

"That's not what I was worried about." Joyce slowly slid off the couch before crawling to the spot next to Abbie. Soon, they were only a few precious inches away from one another. Abbie wasn't about to make a move, though. Not when Joyce was so withdrawn from the world that Christmas. *I still can't believe I couldn't tell what was going on. She hid it so well at first.* Abbie wouldn't begrudge her, though. Not when there was so much at stake in her heart. *Nobody should feel alone at Christmas. Especially if they don't want to feel alone!*

Joyce was special. No, she was more than special. She was *precious*. Every time Abbie looked at her, right here, in the flesh, she was reminded that this was the remarkable woman she happened to meet after a chance click on a website. Wasn't it crazy how soon things could change like that?

"What were you worried about?"

A small smile cracked on the corner of Joyce's mouth. "We might start getting frisky."

Abbie giggled. "Something wrong with that?"

"Well, you know, after last night..."

"Hey." Abbie understood it now. Joyce was probably in a bad head space when they were fooling around the night before. Just as well that it didn't really go anywhere. The first time they actually had sex should be special! *All that means is neither of us is sobbing by the end of it.* Seemed simple enough. "Don't worry about last night. Things happen. I don't want you to feel pressured to do anything you're not into, even if it *is* with me."

Joyce snorted. "I feel the need to keep apologizing. I feel like I've put you so out these past few days. Coming to visit you during a pandemic, for one thing..."

"Um, I was the one who *invited you*."

"...Dumping all of my hot issues on your head. Acting so ungrateful for all that you've done. I mean, look at this place." Joyce craned her head around, taking in the decorations Abbie had thrown together both before and right after her girlfriend arrived. "You didn't do this for me, though. You did it for you, too. As well as you should have. This is also your Christmas, and you don't get to spend it with your family."

"Yeah..." Abbie sighed. "I'll get it over it, though, and there's always next year. Like I kept telling my mother, I'd rather miss it this year than not have her next year. I still deal with the public here and there. It's not a chance worth taking in her condition."

"But you didn't think twice about inviting me, huh?"

"You have a firmer head on your shoulders than my mom. She's run by pure emotion. You? You're logical. You wouldn't have come at my behest unless you thought it would be worth your while. I like that about you, though. Logical."

"I'm not *only* logical." Joyce nudged Abbie's shoulder. "I can be spontaneous and sexy, too. Once you get to know me a little better, I'll be jumping your bones every chance I get."

Sure, she said that all cool and such, but Abbie was instantly intrigued by the prospect. "Like when I come home from work?" She bit her lip. "'Cause that could be pretty hot. Never had something like that before."

"Considering the times, you better wash up first."

"See! Logical!" Abbie slammed her hands down between them, lips coming close to Joyce's cheek. "I wouldn't have thought of that. My pussy would be doing all the talking." Sheesh, talking to Joyce like this in person was still so weird. Should Abbie be embarrassed? *I mean, we always talked like this online.* So free and effortless with monitors between them. Abbie could be whatever suave sex kitten she imagined herself to be. In person, though? She could see the little tweaks to Joyce's personality whenever "sex Abbie" came out. Did she take Abbie seriously? Or did Joyce think her positively lame?

Did it matter?

"I meant what I said back on the beach." *Real nice save, Abs.* Totally change the mood. "I really do love you. You're someone who has become incredibly special to me over these past few months. Never thought I'd meet someone who encompasses my heart like you do. 'Cause it's not only because you're pretty. You're also *so* smart and talented. I've seen your graphic work. My God, I admire you so much for putting up with what you've been through. I can't even imagine being in your shoes. I think I would straight up collapse into a pile of useless mush if I lost my family like that through the years."

Joyce's expression plummeted into the pits of bad memories. "When it happens, you only have two options. Get through it, or succumb. Most people want to live. So they get through it."

"See? I would totally succumb."

"You might surprise yourself. Then again, we can sit here and postulate what might happen all we want, but it doesn't change the fact you don't know until you live through it. Anyway..." Joyce placed her hand on Abbie's. "I'm grateful for you, too. You're a big reason I've made it through this nightmare of a year. I can't even imagine what it would have been like without your smiling face to greet me multiple times a week."

Words like that melted right in Abbie's heart. "You're the sweetest person I've ever met, Joyce Stewart. I think anyone would be amazingly lucky to have you in their family."

"I don't think I've ever heard you call me by my full name before." Joyce chuckled. "Not even my mother did that."

"It's such a nice name. Not like..."

"Abbie Greywood?" Joyce squeezed her hand. "Or should it be *Abbie Griswold.*"

Laughter spilled from Abbie's lips. "When you say my name, it actually sounds nice." She leaned in closer to Joyce. "Say it again."

"Abbie..." Joyce's mouth was now close enough to touch Abbie's. "Greywood."

There were no giggles now. No chuckles. No laughter. Only two women in love, kissing like it was truly their first time.

The fire cackled. Mistletoe hung from the ceiling. The Christmas tree lights twinkled, and the scent of a pumpkin-pine candle filled the air. The more Abbie and Joyce kissed, the more perfect the moment felt.

Abbie was the one to topple first. Instead of falling back on the carpet, however, she fell upon Joyce, who opened her arms to everything her girlfriend offered.

Healing. Love. Comfort and joy. No more expectations. Only what felt right – and hope for their future, together.

Abbie had never felt so blessed on a simple Christmas night.

EPILOGUE

They lucked out with blue skies and a decent breeze that was neither too cold nor not cool *enough* for the physical activity taking place two blocks from the beach. As soon as Joyce awoke that morning, she checked the weather forecast on her phone and hopped out of her sleeping bag with a little skip in her step.

It was the big day. A day big enough to cause her to sell her bed on NextDoor and take a giant leap only a few weeks divorced from Christmas.

Abbie was the one who awoke with a start, though. First thing out of her mouth? "Is it time to get up? Shit. The sun's up. When did the sun come up?

Joyce inhaled a deep breath and grabbed two cans of cold coffee from the fridge. *Can't make hot coffee if you don't have a coffee maker!* Joyce's apartment was mostly bare, aside from the boxes piled up in one corner and the vacuum cleaner she borrowed from a neighbor propped up against the bathroom door. As soon as the boxes were loaded into the U-Haul downstairs, she and Abbie were making for the coast.

The big day had come, after all. The two of them were driving their separate vehicles back to Seaside, and Joyce was starting the next chapter of her life.

The idea to move – let alone into Abbie's house – had not come easily, and they were both even warier about making such a jump so soon. Naturally, the U-Haul jokes wrote themselves, especially when the actual thing was parked in front of her house. Yet Joyce didn't care about stereotypes or wondering if she was making the right decision. Once she realized her lease was up in February and she was in love with Abbie...

Well, there was nothing for her in Portland. Most of her other friends from the "before times" were moving away as well, since there was no point in hanging around an expensive city if there was nowhere to go, nothing to do, and nobody to hang out with – assuming people were minding themselves, that was.

Joyce had been back to Seaside three more times since Christmas. It helped that it was "only" two hours one way, if the traffic and weather was good. *Why spend so much time in my shitty apartment in a cold city when I could be at the beach with my girlfriend?* The video chats had reignited in earnest, but they both agreed that the "real thing" was so much better. *Once the walls came down between us, things got explosive in Abbie's bedroom.* That may have been one reason Joyce was keen to move in with her as soon as her lease was up. Abbie didn't have a problem with it, either. The only barrier was getting the all-clear from her parents, who were definitely unsure at first, considering they had entrusted their summer home to a daughter who had been *single* for so long. Yet it was Abbie's father, Dwayne, who cracked first. *"Oh, come on, honey,"* he had said to his wife over Zoom. *"Abbie's a good girl and Joyce seems like a lovely lady. We can't visit anytime for the next few months. They should be together!"* There was a stipulation, of course. With Joyce bringing in her graphic design income, the Greywoods humbly asked that she chip in with either the mortgage or the property taxes. After Joyce looked at the math, she offered to pay the mortgage on the place. They were so shocked that she readily agreed that she didn't tell them the mortgage was four hundred dollars less than her rent!

Already Joyce was filled with the amazing possibilities this move was going to bring her.

The beach! Every day! No, she wouldn't go every day, but having it so close rejuvenated her desire to become a beach bum for the first time in her life. Abbie promised to show her every great restaurant, gift shop, and sweet person in the area once things were a little more stable in the pandemic department. Until then, she would come help Joyce move the last of her things.

Abbie didn't have a car, but she had a license and – and! – knew how to drive shift. She got behind the wheel of the U-Haul while Joyce made the rounds of her car, ensuring everything, from the trunk to the back doors, was properly closed. Quite the feat, considering how many plastic totes and heavy cloth shopping bags were locked into her trunk and the backseat. The passenger side seat became home to some of her more precious valuables: stuffed animals and dolls from her childhood that she could never quite let go.

The air was cold, but the sky was blue and the roads clear as they traversed Highway 20 between Portland and Seaside. Occasionally, Abbie brought up the rear of their small caravan, but more often that not she became lost between Joyce and a small string of cars that had passed her. Didn't matter. She was always around the bend behind Joyce, and it wasn't like they didn't know where to go once they reached Highway 101.

Joyce hadn't brought a *lot* of furniture, but she had brought some inheritances from her childhood home and her own mother's that the Greywoods agreed made fine pieces in their vacation home. *"Think of it as our home, honestly,"* Abbie told her girlfriend. *"I have my family wrapped around my finger. As long as we take good care of this place, I have a feeling it might be ours one day."* Joyce could hardly believe it, of course. The concept was too good to be true.

Yet she had to admit her grandmother's old antique furniture that had been collecting clothes and dust in a tiny one-bedroom apartment looked damn good in the beachside property. The dark, polished wood complemented the pale yellow walls and white trim of the living and dining rooms. *Have to hand it to my grandma – she had some timeless tastes.*

Sammy did her best to help the couple as they unloaded the U-Haul and prepared to take it back to the local rental center on time. Yet more often than not, a neighbor had to stop by to restrain the excited dog as the couple carried in Joyce's desk, soon to make its home by the front window in the living room. The space was tight, but soon she'd have a fabulous view of the street with the couch right behind her. She may have mentioned getting a cat. To her delight, Abbie was into the idea. Sammy always needed new friends, after all.

Since it was still winter, the sun went down too early. They ate a takeout dinner before Joyce went back into their bedroom and began unpacking more of her clothes.

Abbie happened to walk in the moment Joyce unearthed something that she hadn't properly unpacked the *last* time she moved.

"What is it?" She had caught her girlfriend holding a ratty stuffed cat that had long seen better days. "Some old toy?"

Joyce held up the white cat, with its inflated tail and eyes completely covered by matted, dirty "fur." "I can't believe I forgot about this! My best friend when I was a little kid. This is Kitty. My mom says she got her for me when she happened to be in the hardware store one day and decided I had to have it. From that day on, it was my favorite toy in the world. The one thing I would grab in a house fire." She clutched the toy to her chest. If she nuzzled her nose against the scalp? *I can smell my childhood.* More like fabric softener and soap she had used to try to get out thirty-year-old grime. "Man, it's been years since I last slept with her. She doesn't look so great right now, though..." Joyce sighed. "I remember. Know how I told you I used to get head lice as a kid? One year I got them so bad that nothing was working. My mom had to go totally nuclear on the house. That included throwing *all* of my stuffed animals into the dryer. She didn't protect them in any way. To top it off? They were supposed to stay in a garbage bag for *six months.* I used to joke those were the months I grew up." She had been way too young for that. Only eight. Or maybe nine. "When I finally got to unwrap them, they looked like this. Never the same."

Abbie cupped her hands beneath her girlfriend's hands and gently took Kitty away. "She's adorable."

"You think so?"

"I can tell she was well loved over the years. I'd love to see your other stuffed animals you've got there, too."

Joyce couldn't explain why that put such a smile on her face and a frolic in her heart. *Someone who appreciates my childhood and wants to hear my stories...* She had a million of them. Stories she had never told anyone else, because there had never been anyone to tell. Now?

"How about we go to sleep early tonight?" Abbie said. "Let's get up a little early and go for a walk on the beach before breakfast. Maybe it can become one of our routines." Her hand soon took Joyce's. "Every time we go for a walk, you can tell me a story. Any story. About your mom. Your old house. When you went to school..."

It sounded cheesy, didn't it? Yet Joyce had to hold back the tears. *Stories I kept inside of me for so long.* Some of them she had almost forgotten, like Kitty getting thrown in the dryer because she might have been covered in creepy little critters. Joyce took her stuffed animal back into her arms and hugged her as if she were once again seven.

Later, as Abbie got ready for bed and saw to Sammy's last minute needs, Joyce unpacked one small box full of framed photos she had kept over the years. *My grandpa and me. My mom and her older brothers back in the fifties. My grandparents' wedding...* Things she savored, because somebody had to, and it might as well be her.

Then?

Her mother's graduation photo, c. 1969.

The beehive was in and every late sixties beauty wore a black dress for her most essential photo. Seeing her mother so young, back in the prime of her life before age and stress brought her down, was always so surreal. Joyce looked like her. Or was it the other way around?

Joyce took it out into the living room and placed it on her desk, now properly positioned in front of the living room window. She looked out into the night, the clear sky full of twinkling stars. If Joyce pressed her ear against the glass, she heard the not-so-faraway rumblings of the ocean. If she blocked out every thought, she heard her mother's voice on the wind.

"I love you, joy of my heart. Be happy."

"Joyce!"

She turned around to find Abbie standing by the hallway. "Sorry! I was lost in my thoughts."

Abbie chuckled. "You coming to bed?"

"Be right there."

Abbie disappeared into the bedroom, dog at her feet.

Joyce released the breath she had been holding since Abbie startled her. Now that she was back in the real world, she relaxed. Here she was. In the present. No Christmas decorations, but the promise of a brand-new year full of much more cheer than she had anticipated the year before.

I was with her for Christmas. Abbie turned off the lights on her way into the hallway. *Now she's with me for the rest of my life.*

Maybe that was why her mother was finally ready to depart the mortal world. She knew Joyce was well taken care of now.

For one moment, that made Joyce feel the safest she had been in years. The next moment? *I better make sure I'm taking care of Abbie, too!*

She rushed into the bedroom, where she found Abbie sitting on the edge of the bed. Soon, they were tackling one another and laughing like *this* would be their nightly bedtime routine.

Joyce had never been so excited for the rest of her life.

Hildred Billings is a Japanese and Religious Studies graduate who has spent her entire life knowing she would write for a living someday. She has lived in Japan a total of three times in three different locations, from the heights of the Japanese alps to the hectic Tokyo suburbs, with a life in Shikoku somewhere in there too. When she's not writing, however, she spends most of her time talking about Asian pop music, cats, and bad 80's fantasy movies with anyone who will listen...or not.

Her writing centers around themes of redemption, sexuality, and death, sometimes all at once. Although she enjoys writing in the genre of fantasy the most, she strives to show as much reality as possible through her characters and situations, since she's a furious realist herself.

Currently, Hildred lives in Oregon with her girlfriend, with dreams of maybe having a cat around someday.

Connect with Hildred on any of the following:

Website: http://www.hildred-billings.com
Twitter: http://twitter.com/hildred
Facebook: http://facebook.com/authorhildredbillings
Tumblr: http://tumblr.com/hildred